364/
700

Secrets of the Flock

J.B.BROWNE

That y... for
helping the World's
poor by buying this
book . J. B. Browne.

Instagram:
ewe_chunners

Dedication

For Barbara, who preferred to be called flockmistress, and for Nicky who died too young.

Secrets of the Flock

J B Browne

Rough Fell Books

British Library Cataloguing in Publication Data
A catalogue record for this book is available from the British Library

ISBN 978-1-9164287-0-6

Typeset by Amolibros, Milverton, Somerset
www.amolibros.co.uk
This book production has been managed by Amolibros
Printed and bound by T J International Ltd, Padstow, Cornwall, UK

1: A lamb is born

Wednesday 13th January

The ewe chunners. Birth is near. She twists her head skyward and chunners again. Out here in the field the wind is cold; the ewe has little protection, and her lambs will have even less. As her womb contracts and her uterus dilates, her maternal instincts are rippling through her body and her chunnering has begun. It is a noise that comes from deep within. It is the call she makes now her lambs are about to arrive. It is the call of a mother.

This lamb is early. She should not be giving birth until March, when the spring arrives. But a gate left carelessly open and a wandering ram means that she is due to give birth out in the raw weather high in the Newlands Valley. On a clear day the view from the field, where her body is twisting with contractions, is stunning. You can see the mass of Skiddaw, Carl Side, Dodd and Latrigg. The ewe knows none of this. All she knows is that it is night time. If her lamb is born in this mud and in this cold it will not survive.

She chunners again. Birth is near. Across at the farmhouse the outside light goes on. The door opens and a figure emerges, well-wrapped against the cold. It is time for the evening check of the flock. This is the shepherdess. She is the one on whom the

1

sixty ewes depend every day, just like she depends on them. As she emerges, a collie darts around her heels, followed more slowly by a black and tan mongrel. The collie, like the shepherdess, is not in her prime, but for both of them the instinct to tend, to herd, to corral remains strong. So at night, when most people are on their way to bed or watching the evening news, this trio are doing their late evening check. And it is this routine that might save the life of the ewe or her lamb.

Across the field the torch beam shines and instinctively the shepherdess knows that something is wrong. As the collie approaches, most ewes run. The only time they don't is when the maternal instinct overrides the animal instinct to flee. The ewe in the middle of the field stands her ground. The dog stops, knowing that an unspoken rule of its world has been broken. The shepherdess knows that the ewe must be about to give birth or has just done so. She fetches a rope to guide the ewe inside. In the field, the ewe and the dog have not moved when she returns.

She gently places the rope round the ewe's neck. Normally she would have to herd the ewe first, drive it in a corner or use her dog to push it towards the barn. The ewe is led into a small pen and the shepherdess lays down straw and fetches water. She boils the kettle and lays out the towels for lambing. She turns on the radio for company. As a shepherdess, as a flock mistress, she knows she has to wait for whatever happens next. So in a cold barn on the high slopes of the Newlands Valley under the shadows of Catbells and Maiden Moor, beneath the slopes of High Pike and Robinson, she waits.

As she waits, the shepherdess can be seen under the lights of the barn. She is in a boiler suit, tight under the arms, ripped in the legs and covered in the soil and shit of farm life. Her boots and her face bear the imprint of a life spent hill farming. Her hair is grey with the last vestiges of a perm. Her eyes are tired, but shining. She loves and lives for the sheep that depend on her and now one of her flock, one of her favourites, is giving birth. Looking closer, it's clear that she was once beautiful. Take away the wrinkles and the grey hair, smooth away the exhaustion and a couple of extra pounds gained from a life alone – in her youth, when her looks and her self-esteem were much better, she would have turned heads. But now it is only the dogs and sheep that look twice when she is near.

She waits and watches the ewe, timing the contractions. After half an hour with no progress, she knows that she must check the ewe to see whether the head is emerging. Inside the womb a lamb sits in a sac. Its front feet and the tip of its nose should push the jaws of the womb apart, so that as the ewe pushes, the lamb emerges. If she is to be soon back in bed, she wants to be able to see just the tip of a lamb's nose and two feet close behind. If she sees anything much else, the ewe will be in trouble and her night will be long.

She lifts the ewe's tail and gently places her finger on the opening to the womb. There is mucus but no nose and no feet to be felt. She pushes her fingers further in through the cervix and eventually finds the blunt outline of a tail and a rear end. She lets out a low groan of despair, for the lamb is breach and must be turned around. With her arthritic knuckles and her stiff fingers this is the worst kind of birth. She can't grip as well and she can't turn the lamb as easily as she would have done a decade earlier.

This is a favourite ewe, a ewe who greets her when she enters the barn, who nibbles her fingers when she has food and feeds from her hand. This is a ewe that makes her feel wanted, needed. So she must get the lamb out alive, by turning the lamb round and pulling it out nose out first.

She ties the ewe's head to the side of the pen so that it cannot move. As she does so, the midnight news comes on. She knows she needs to get the lamb out within an hour or it will be crushed by the ewe's contractions that are meant to push it out.

She pushes her hand into the ewe's womb. She is up to her elbow as she searches for the slippery lamb's head in the dark of the womb. Her fingers feel for the head and she finds it. She now has to turn the head and the legs together, for if a leg is left behind the shoulder joint, it will act like a door wedge. It is like turning a car around in a parking space barely as long as it is wide. She gathers the foot together with the head in preparation for turning.

Something is not right. The leg she has found is at the wrong angle. Is it a back leg? She feels up the leg and she definitely has a front leg. Realisation dawns on her and she yells a single 'No!' – to the cold night, at the weather man reading the news, to the dog who is watching her from a bale of straw. She shouts again; a single dejected desolate word: 'Twins!' She has found the front leg of a second lamb.

She pauses. It is now 12.30 a.m. She reaches into the womb again, this time above her elbow. The ewe is restless and the contractions close around her arm like the toothless jaws of a giant mouth. She finds the head again and feels down to track the missing front legs. She locates one and pushes it up towards the head. She now tries to turn the lamb over and push her hand down the other side to track the other front leg. Her hands are weak and she feels the leg slip out of her hand. She tries again with a firmer grasp and this time, she succeeds.

Now she takes the two legs and the nose in her hand and tries to turn the head gently round. The world service news starts at 1 a.m. She has been at this one manoeuvre for half an hour. She is exhausted and covered in the fluids of birth. Her arm aches and the nose slips from her fingers. She reaches in again and pulls again. She wants to yank the head. She wants to vent her anger on the lamb and the ewe and the world for her feeling of sheer powerlessness against the force of a single sheep's womb.

Gradually, she pulls the nose round and the legs with it. It takes all her strength. She is weeping now, with exhaustion, and with frustration. She feels like it is hopeless. Just as she feels she can do no more, the nose slowly comes round. She feels the kicking of the lamb, as it is now twisted back on itself. But after she has pulled for more than ten minutes, suddenly the lamb wriggles under her hand and is the right way around. She yells with joy. Her fingers ache, her arms ache and she sobs again. The dog, her loyal sidekick, seeing her distress comes to lick her face through the bars of the pen. The ewe chunners. Now the nose and the front legs are peeking out through the opening to the womb. 'Push!' she shouts to the lamb. 'Push!' she repeats, more gently this time – this ewe is almost like a pet to her. The head begins to emerge, closely followed by the front feet. She can see the tongue poking out between the lamb's lips – it is blue, meaning that the lamb is short of oxygen. She hovers round the ewe, concerned. The birth has gone on for too long and she must intervene again. She takes the front legs and gently starts to pull them as the ewe pushes and chunners. The lamb is half out now – and then, all at once, falls like jelly off a table onto the floor. The lamb is born. The shepherdess yells with delight but then stops. The lamb isn't wriggling or breathing.

She kneels down and pulls the mucus away from the lamb's mouth. She pummels its tiny chest. No response. She has no choice but to swing the lamb. Her hands are tired, her knuckles ache, and she could lie down in the straw and sleep without hesitation. She fantasises about a hot bath and a whisky, but she knows she must carry on. She picks up the lamb by its back legs, cleans the mucus from its legs and, just as she is about to take the risk of swinging the lamb, it coughs. It coughs.

'You beauty,' she tells it. It now takes gulping breaths – it even lifts its head up and voicelessly bleats. The ewe responds with another chunner and the shepherdess releases its head from the rope that was tying it to the side of the pen. The ewe chunners, and turns to lick the lamb, which weakly bleats again.

She had almost forgotten. There is a second lamb. As the first lamb and its mother continue their bonding, she peeks beneath the tail again and pushes her finger gently inside. She can feel no nose, no feet. Her legs weaken; she doesn't have the energy to turn another lamb around. She decides to wait twenty minutes. She returns across the yard to the house to make a cup of tea. It is now past 1.30 a.m. The stars are out as she crosses the yard, but she doesn't notice. The frost is forming in the still air. The dog follows at her heels. Her thoughts are focused on tea, chocolate, a whisky and a pee.

The farmhouse has all the hallmarks of a person living alone. The kitchen is the heart of her home with a large Aga in a vast chimney breast. She moves to the sink, pushes aside the detritus of sheep and single living, and washes her hands. She fills the kettle and, boots still on, crosses the living room carpet to the loo. Her bladder relieved and her kettle boiled, she makes the tea. She reaches for her chocolate supply, then for a glass, and pours herself a large measure of whisky. Whisky and chocolate are the diet of the midnight hours.

Fortified, she is ready to return to the sheep shed to see if the second lamb has progressed. She then realises that she cannot carry both the tea and the whisky back to the shed. She looks first at one, then the other. Were she not so tired she would have got a tray or have left the whisky for a nightcap, but she is exhausted. She looks again at the cup and the glass and then pours the whisky into the tea and sets off for the sheep shed, munching on a mouthful of chocolate. This was meant to be an evening where she got an early night.

Back in the sheep shed, the ewe is nuzzling her newfound charge. The lamb is now on its feet, searching in its first tentative steps for food. She puts the tea down and steps into the pen. She holds the ewe's head and reaches down with her other hand and finds her teats. She pummels the udder gently and then squeezes the teat again and feels a squirt of milk on her hand. She pushes the lamb towards the teat. She then moves behind the ewe to see what progress there is with the second lamb.

There is still no sign of improvement. She sits on a hay bale and waits and drinks from her cup. She gags on the taste of tea with whisky but can feel the warmth filling her insides as she swallows. As she sits and waits, her thoughts drift. Encouraged by the alcohol, her exhaustion and the chocolate, she remembers her own children. She remembers the pain she felt in labour, she remembers her husband and how he wasn't there for the birth, she remembers the first child whom she miscarried, she remembers the birth of her third child and how labour never seemed to end when her daughter's head was too big. She remembers the tearing as she gave a final, enormous push, and how she couldn't pee properly for months afterwards. She remembers all the pain of childbirth, all the sleepless nights and the scars that didn't heal, caused by the daughter she now so rarely sees. All these thoughts, in the time it takes her to gulp down her tea.

She checks the ewe again and now the contractions have done their work. The nose and the two front legs are poking out. She debates with herself whether she should help, but it is not a difficult decision. The time is now way past 2 a.m. and she is too tired to keep doing nothing. She gently pulls the front legs and the head emerges. She tugs each leg one after the other. The lamb is now halfway out, but she can see it has a blue tongue so she quickly pulls it the rest of the way out. Its sibling is now quite perky and searching for the teat, stumbling across the straw, oblivious of the inert figure on the ground beside it.

She clears the mucus from its mouth. She shouts at it, 'Live! Live!' Once more, she pummels its chest and rubs it frantically with straw. She shows it to the ewe and lets her sniff it. She doesn't want the mother to reject it by the morning because she has not bonded with it. She pummels it again.

It is smaller than the first born; she has no choice. She climbs out of the pen and grabs a towel, and then picks up the lamb out by its back legs. And then, as if she is practising for the discus, she stands feet astride in the open barn and swings the lamb in a vast circle floor to ceiling to floor. After three whole loops she has energy for no more. The lamb's lungs should be cleared and its blood circulated. She drops the lamb back in the pen with its mother. The shepherdess knows that she has nothing more to give. If the pummelling, the pounding and the swinging have not brought the lamb back from the brink, then there is no more that she can do.

But it has worked. The lamb starts to breathe as its mother licks it. Its heart beats and its tiny chest rises and falls. The ewe chunners. This noise, this call that is reserved just for the newborn lamb, is the noise of a mother. The shepherdess finally smiles. She checks that the ewe has water and fresh straw, turns off the radio, and calls the dogs. It is just before 3 a.m.; time for bed.

She reaches the farmhouse, locks the door and heads upstairs. Only in her bedroom does she remove her boots. As she sits on her bed, she cries again; cries that she has two lambs, cries with exhaustion and cries for the children to whom she gave birth, and whom now she hardly ever sees. For a moment, just a moment, she lies back on the bed and in that moment falls asleep.

At 6 a.m. the alarm goes, and the shepherdess is still fully clothed, asleep on her bed. And, out in the sheep shed, the ewe licks and paws at the body of the second-born lamb. It has died in the night.

2: Talking to someone

Tuesday 26th January

The potatoes get eaten last, saved on the plate until the rest of the food is gone. They are then consumed, relished, savoured as the final act of a meal. They are the small treat, the most token of delicacies where each of the few pleasures must be savoured. In a world where there is neither cake nor icing and where potatoes are a treat to be treasured, it is better not to raise hope or move beyond the subservience to small expectations.

The potato-savourer is a wiry, pale man. He has short hair, cropped close to his head. He is neither handsome nor ugly. Looking into his eyes, they aren't shining, but numb. They are the eyes which come from years of surviving.

This man is not a hen-pecked husband or a homeless rough sleeper or a migrant labourer. He could be all of those things. But he is a prisoner, a lifer. The state will own a part of him for as long as he lives. Right now, they own every move he makes. He is in a small open prison, Fellview, tucked under the escarpment of the far western fells of the Lake District in Lorton Vale. The state has owned him for the last twelve years, ever since he was nineteen.

He started at a prison on the Isle of Wight, and for two years his life belonged not to the state, but to whoever led the top prison gang. His youth and his skinny muscled body meant that he was used and rented for sex. If he resisted, he was beaten. And with every beating, the parameters of joy and sadness, of hope and disappointment, moved closer together. Now, after twelve years of prison, he is subservient to whatever he needs to be subservient to. Once the meal is finished, once the last potato is gone, then he will be subservient to the needs of the prison psychologist.

After twelve years inside, he is in an open prison where he is being evaluated for release. He could be allowed the first dose of freedom by going out a day each week for community work, but first the new psychologist must evaluate him, to see if he is ready.

In the small office there are two chairs and a low coffee table laid out in an attempt at intimacy for the psychologist to encourage prisoners to talk. It's a room made to seem like an office anywhere, except for the lack of anything on the walls, or, for that matter, any coffee on the coffee table.

'Tell me your story,' says the psychologist.

The prisoner has told this story so many times while in prison. Each time, he has given a little more of what his inquisitors want to hear. Each time, he has tried to work out how to sound contrite without sounding compliant. If he is too perfect in his answers, they will believe he is faking his sorrow. As he gets closer to a possible date for being let out on licence he also knows he needs the psychologist's evaluation to be good.

In his mind, he sees the stage. He imagines the audience, the lights bright in his eyes, the other actors hushed, for this is his great speech, his monologue. He imagines himself as one of his favourite actors. Who will he be today? Clint Eastwood? George Clooney? Johnny Depp? He senses that this psychologist would not appreciate the nervous tics and laughs of Depp. Instead, he settles for James McAvoy.

So he begins.

'I was seventeen, maybe eighteen, when I met this girl. I was working as a junior in an accountant's firm. I didn't want to be there. It was a compromise with my parents. I wanted to go to university. I had good A levels. I did well at school. I wanted to leave the suffocation of home.

'My parents didn't want me to go to uni. They believed in getting a job and a career. They thought uni was an expensive waste.

'My mother in particular went on and on about it. My older sisters had got jobs and met "nice men", and I should do the same and a meet a "nice woman". Status and "doing the right thing" were everything to her. We sort of agreed that being a trainee accountant might be something we could both live with. A way I could "make something of myself" she said, again and again. I couldn't persuade her that university might really be the way to do that. She only seemed to care about what the neighbours and family though, what her status in the world was. I was just a pawn in her plans.

'So I started in the local accountant as a trainee. There was a group of us, and we would go out for lunch for a sandwich, to the shop in the high street. This girl was serving there when I went down most days. I was the newest, the most junior trainee accountant, and she was good-looking, so we started up the banter. Asking her questions, stuff like that. The lads in the office were all in competition, each trying to eke out of her an extra compliment, an extra-large portion, something which would make us the favourite.

'She would joke back and ask us why we were such eggheads,

or tell us how boring accountants were. One day she said in front of the others that she had made me a bigger sandwich because I looked like I needed feeding up. The others laughed. All this continued for weeks. Then one day as I was eating my lunch I looked at my sandwich wrapper. There it was – a message from her "Call me" and her home phone number. I stopped chewing and then realised that I couldn't let the others know, so I finished the sandwich and made a mental note of her number. That evening I rang her at home. This was before most people had mobile phones. Her mum answered. I realised that I didn't even know her name, so I asked for the girl who worked in the sandwich shop and she came to the phone. She was called Kylie.

'Looking back I should have realised, I should have seen that Kylie was always in control. She picked me as the weakest, the most innocent. From the very first meeting she played the lead. She made the first move. She suggested we meet down a pub the next night and the night after that we had our first kiss and she made the move on me then, too. We stood outside the pub and I said goodnight and she coyly said, "Is that all I get? Come here," and her tongue was in my mouth.'

The pretty psychologist makes notes. The monologue, now almost word perfect, continues. Were she to look up, she would see that he has stopped fidgeting. He is calm. This is not emotional release, but regurgitated script.

'How did the baby happen?' The psychologist asks, looking at her watch.

For a moment he is about to be rude, to be male, and to ruin his act of repentance. But he doesn't say, 'Would you like me to show you?' Instead, he restarts the monologue.

'Bravado, I guess. Flattery. Stupidity. Innocence. What words would you like?'

The psychologist looks up.

The prisoner has changed. For him, his years in prison have not been a waste, but instead the opportunity to read, the opportunity to become chameleon-like. It's the university he never went to. To the other prisoners, his northern accent is the same as ever but to the prison staff, he practises the words and vocabulary he has learned, like a holiday maker practising his French.

'For most young men, sex and the opposite sex, are the main source of kudos and conversation. I was "shagging" the sandwich girl – again, she wanted it, she was happy to lie back in my car and let me lose my virginity, though I doubt she lost hers in the back of that car. I was careless. Stupid, so so stupid. I thought she would take precautions – she didn't. And so, a baby was made in the back of a car. She didn't want to have an abortion and I agreed to stay with her.

'When the baby was born, I was just nineteen. Nobody should have a baby at nineteen. I think, looking back, that I was under her spell. Even during pregnancy we still had sex – still in the back of my car. We had nowhere else to go. Her mum was horrified at her daughter having a baby. She was too young. We were too young, too inexperienced, too innocent. I lived with my parents and they, too, were horrified. My mother was absolutely mortified. We had to "do things properly" – get married and then have the baby.

'We got married two weeks before she gave birth. My mother was happy, in her own deluded way. We finally found us a flat, with help from both sets of parents. When the baby was born, everything changed. Before the birth, she wanted me; maybe it was just for sex, I don't know, but she wanted me. But after the birth, I was a spare part. Our two mothers descended on our flat to help. We were starting a little family and we were "doing the right thing". Now the baby was here, they were grandmothers, and they were besotted. The two grandmothers and Kylie were like three wicked witches. Talking about babies, about breast-feeding, about baby clothes, about nappies, about baby poo, and then about her smile, her gurgles, her noises.

'I began to have dreams. I began to have this recurring dream about being a penis on legs. I would try and do things but couldn't because I had no arms. I was useless. She would then make me have sex in my dreams and I would be inside her, suffocating, claustrophobic, desperate to breathe.'

He notes with satisfaction that this extra nugget has resulted in double underlining from the psychologist.

'And when the grandmothers had gone home and left us alone, I tried to help, but she kept telling me I was useless. I tried to help with cleaning and with the house. It was no good. Everything I did she threw back in my face. I bought her flowers but she threw them on the floor and told me that a few miserable flowers were no compensation for getting her pregnant. It made no sense to me. She didn't have to have the baby. She chose to have it. So why was she so angry with me?

'The flat was tiny. When we argued there was nowhere to go, so I went out. I started drinking with my accountancy mates more and more. I would come back late and she would be there, ready to scream at me. To tell me how useless I was. To tell me how the sex we had was terrible. She knew every button to press in me to make me feel bad about what I had done. Pretty rich, when it was her who led me on.

'One night, I came home late. My mother was meant to be visiting us, to help with the baby, to give Kylie a bit of a break. My work mates had been teasing me. Asking how my sex life was after the baby. I said nothing – but I didn't need to say anything. They knew what to say to wind me up. I don't know whether I had a pint or two extra. I came back full of anger. Anger with my mother for all her snobbery. Angry with Kylie for the situation we were in. I wanted a good argument with somebody. I got home and came through our front door ready for a good shouting match.'

The psychologist's mobile vibrates on the desk between them. The psychologist ignores it. A moment later it rings again. She turns the screen over and looks at it.

'I am sorry, I have to get this. It's my child's nursery. He's only been there a few days.'

'Hello...Yes, that's me...He's been sick! Oh dear. He looked fine this morning.' She blushes and tugs her ear as she says this. 'He needs to be taken out as soon as possible? I see. Have you tried my partner...? No no, of course, he's away at the moment.' There's another pause, and she mouths, 'I am so sorry,' across the room.

'So he needs to be collected as soon as possible. I see. Okay, I will get there as soon as I can. It's at least an hour's drive to get to you...Yes, I'll hurry. No, I realise you don't want him infecting other children.'

She puts the phone down.

'I am so sorry...' she pauses and looks at her notes, '...Stephen, I am going to have go and pick up my child from nursery. They are very strict when a child is ill. We will have to pick this up another time so I will see you when I am back in a few weeks. I really am very sorry.'

Flustered, the psychologist gathers her stuff and the session ends. He has no chance to tell her he prefers the name Steve, but that the system has him down as Stephen and so within the system Stephen he will remain. But after twelve years of institutional life, he knows that inside is the seed of a new life. He is ready to move on. He has done his time. The man who will leave prison is not the man who entered it.

So when in a few days' time he is told that he can start on a day release programme, he scours the notice boards for the different opportunities through which he can escape prison life – if only for a few hours.

3: The end of an era

Friday 12th February

The schoolboy has walked this route every day to school for the last five years or more, but this is the last time he will do so. And so he stops and looks up. He has never really looked at this vast, gleaming white church before. It is the 'Christ Church at Spitalfields', he reads on the sign. It has stood here for 300 years, while the world around has changed it has witnessed much. Round the back, Jack the Ripper despatched one of his victims. It has witnessed the waves of immigration and withstood the bombs of war. And now, after five years, he is suddenly curious, and goes inside.

Here in the east end, in Spitalfields and Bethnal Green, he has lived his entire life, but all that is about to change. His mother is taking him and his sister, far, far away. From the city to the countryside, from the south to the north, from London to the Lake District. In his heart he knows they must go. He has seen his mother suffer too much. They need to move.

Suddenly, this makes him nostalgic for all the things he has taken for granted. So, on his last day, he is now out on a last sentimental walk home. He has just left his mates for the last time.

These are teenage boys so there are no tears, no hugs, no speeches, just a final 'see ya' and they are gone. Two friends he has walked with every day to and from school, and with two words of farewell they are gone. They will keep in touch on Facebook, perhaps.

He stands outside Christ Church. He has had an emotional day. His favourite teacher, not that he would ever admit it, stopped him at the end of the final history class together.

'You owe me that essay on the policy of appeasement,' the teacher said. 'Don't suppose I'll ever get it now.'

'I'll post it to you,' the boy offered.

'Don't bother,' the history teacher replied, 'but do something for me, Ashley. Make something of your life. I have had hundreds of boys and girls who have come through these doors over the years who listen to what I teach them about Hitler, and the Treaty of Versailles, about China and Mao. And most of them…'

'Will this take long, sir?' the boy interrupts with a grin.

'Consider this the detention I should have given you a dozen times…and many of them do their best. They listen hard – some of them. They do their homework. But I know you are different. I have rarely seen such potential wrapped tight in the clothes of laziness and indifference. When you put your brain into gear, Ashley, when you apply yourself, you grasp these things with such speed and such energy it's frightening. Even among A Level pupils, you are the hare and most of the others are tortoises.

'So one day you will wake up and finally decide to try, when your brain is finally allowed to have a decent bit of exercise, you will be able to do amazing things.'

'I'll invite you to my graduation, sir.'

'You can mock, but just remember the words "amazing things". You have great potential; this is your new start. The Lakes are beautiful. Keswick School is excellent, and their sixth form is very good, I hear. So start again; be someone different. Make it happen. Goodbye.'

'Goodbye, sir, and thank you.' Leaving his flippant tone aside for once he continues, 'I have enjoyed your lessons more than anything. Really.'

'That means a lot,' the teacher answers. 'That means a lot.'

Yet it is not leaving school which fills his thoughts now. It is leaving home. It is the scene from one night two months ago, which set this move north in motion.

It was late at night and he had just gone to bed. His stepdad Roberto – his mum always encourages Ashley to call him 'Dad' and he does to please her, but only out loud – came home from the pub. He heard him downstairs. He knows his mother hates it when Roberto drinks too much, and as so often, he heard their raised voices. Usually these arguments last only a few minutes, even a few seconds, but it was different on this night. As he listened, there was a noise he couldn't identify and then silence. Then he realised that he could hear his mother crying.

There is always tension when his stepdad Roberto is around, and that has been the case for as long as he can remember. On the good days, he is charming, full of generosity and smiles. On these days, the whole family can relax. But on the bad days, he is full of anger and rage, and the whole family is tense.

They try to hide all this from his little sister Emily. She is her mother's golden girl. Even Ashley treats her with a gentleness he never shows his mother. His sister is all pink and Barbie. She turned twelve on her last birthday and is in the first year at secondary school. She is five years younger than her seventeen-year-old brother and in all manner of ways there is a gulf between them; boy versus girl, sporty versus ballet, quiet versus chatty, dark frizzy hair versus blond curls. But he, like his mother, is very protective of her.

There are peaks and troughs, ebbs and flows, of the mood, of the level of tension in the house. The worst times are always at the end of the day when Roberto is drunk. As he has got older, he has seen more of 'his dad': drunk, rude, lecherous, with the stare of a man for whom drink has uncovered his real feelings.

His mother always tries to make sure that his sister is in bed well before his dad gets home. This is just a part of life. When Roberto comes in he always wants to say goodnight to her. His mum always says, 'No, she is asleep.'

Sometimes he insists on going up, too drunk to see sense. His mother always accompanies him around her, a ewe protecting her lambs from threats. When she cannot prevent these late night bouts of leering goodnights, she watches as her swaying, stubble-chinned, stinking-breathed partner kisses his daughter goodnight.

Years later, when they were both old enough to have children of their own, his sister tells him that she learnt not to 'wake up' when he came visiting. Whatever else happened, she would pretend to be asleep. For if she stirred, if she moved, he would only kiss her more and his hands would move to places that they shouldn't. Years later, Emily told her big brother that she lay in bed some nights if she was not quite asleep, hearing him come back and dreading hearing the steps on the stairs. On some nights, she wet the bed in fear of his visits. Her mother just changed the bed without comment.

Christmas was the worst time, she said, because the fragile routine was changed. Roberto would stay home and she would stay up later. So at Christmas, and other holidays, it became impossible to avoid him. And so Christmas, an event that should have been the happiest of times for a young girl growing up, became a time to dread.

But that night, back before he knew all this, he heard his

parents arguing downstairs and hoped the noise wouldn't wake her. His mother's crying didn't stop and he lay there, listening to her tears.

This is not right, he thought.

He got out of bed and paused at the top of the stairs. The crying continued and he silently went downstairs. He paused again in the hall. Peering round the living room door, the sight that greeted him nearly made him scream. All he could see was Roberto's bare buttocks and his trousers round his ankles. No child likes to imagine, let alone see, their parents having sex, but it was his mother's face that shocked him. Her eyes were screwed tight shut and she was crying. One eye was swollen, and the skin all around was bruised and bloody. On her lip, she had a large cut and there were spots of blood on the pale carpet, on her blouse, and on her face.

In an instant, he knew this was not making love, not sex, not right. For a few seconds more, he watched this man's buttocks rise and fall, and watched his beer-breathed head try to kiss her neck. For a moment, Ashley froze. But then, all of a sudden, he felt enraged. His mother was suffering things he never realised to try and hold their family together.

No more, he thought.

He rushed to the kitchen and grabbed the heaviest saucepan he could find. An imperfect weapon, but it would have to do. He then went back into the living room and towered over them before they even realised he was there.

Roberto looked up a split-second before the saucepan hit him. As his mother screamed 'No!' he brought the saucepan down on his head and knocked him unconscious.

The next morning, nothing was said, but when he got home from school his mother told him Roberto had moved out, and that they were moving north as soon as they could. She told him that an old friend said that she has plenty of work she could do.

The suddenness, the ferocity of this change, surprised even him. He had never seen his mother that determined, that steely, and he knew his life was about to change.

By the end of the February half term, they are settling into a small rented house in Portinscale, just outside of Keswick, in the Lake District.

4: A first day out

Saturday 13th February

Far below, a small figure toils on a bicycle up the long hill out of Buttermere and into the Newlands Valley. The climb from the tiny chapel past the ancient oaks and up to the summit of the pass at Swinside Gill is just a mile. On a bicycle, it is a long hard climb to the pass.

This is no ordinary cyclist and no ordinary journey. Passers-by will just see a normal thirty-something man working hard to climb the long hill. Most will mistake his dull clothes and ancient bike as the hallmarks of an enthusiastic but impoverished Lake District lover. But they would be wrong. It is a murderer climbing up this long hill of penitence, remorse and retribution. This is Steve on his first trial of a new day release assignment from the Fellview open prison. He has been out before on day release, but not on his own, and only to a business.

The prison has made the arrangements and now he is going to do work placement with a local farmer. The prison has checked the suitability of the assignment with the prisoner. He is assessed low risk on account of his behaviour. He wouldn't be allowed to work with children, though, but will just help with the livestock and farm work. He will be the farm hand and he will have meals with the farmer and his family. This is all part of the journey he must make back to the real world.

Inside he has butterflies. What if they ask him what he did? What if they ask him to describe his crimes, or ask about his family? Steve has been told he must answer. This is part of the process, they say. This is easy to say, but hard to do. He has thought about this day for years; this is as close to freedom as Steve has been for twelve years.

As he climbs, he looks back the way he has come and sees the rain clouds gathering. When he reaches the summit, he stops. He stops and stands next to his bike and just turns around and around. He looks at the hills whose names he doesn't know. Before prison he cared nothing for the outdoors, for hills, for nature, but now, as he stands dwarfed by the grandeur, he feels the first twitch, the first stirring of what life after prison might hold.

He is not fit. Not fit for cycling at least; he cannot remember when he last cycled. Not since he began his prison sentence, anyway, so this bicycle ride has left him exhausted. He wonders why the prison did not arrange for him to be given a lift.

He has reached the summit and it is now downhill. He freewheels, not pedalling, not slowing himself, till he loses his nerve and brakes. His hair is blown by the slipstream. He takes the curves and potholes and camber of the single track road at speed. He dodges a ewe and its lamb, which stare at him, reluctant to move out of the road. This is freedom and, after twelve years of institutional life, the small liberty of riding a bike at the speed he chooses is exhilarating.

At the second road junction, he stops. He looks at his instructions and takes the right fork. The road is gentler now and the hedgerows are closed in on either side. At the next junction, he turns left and soon sees the sign to New Turn Farm. He walks the bicycle slowly up the gravel and dirt drive. He is nervous now. He imagines the farmer, imagines him as a big man with a ruddy complexion, can almost hear his thick accent and his large hands.

He knocks on the farmhouse door and waits. This is raw freedom, the ability to be terrified on the doorstep of a stranger's house. The door opens and a woman stands on the threshold.

'Hello, I'm looking for the farmer.'

'Yes, welcome. I've been expecting you.'

There is an awkward pause. He glances at the instructions from the prison and tries again.

'I am from…er…Fellview…I have come to start my day release. I am looking for J. Chester, the farmer.'

'Yes, welcome. I've been expecting you.'

Even this introduction does not make him realise, and it shows on his face. So the woman adds, 'I am Joyce Chester, the farmer. It is me you have come to see.'

'You are the farmer. You are the farmer,' he adds, as if to emphasise the point. 'I wasn't expecting that.'

'I can see that,' she retorts. 'Women are farmers too. Come in and have a coffee.'

He enters her kitchen and looks around. It is large, old, and dirty with the mix of farm and domestic life. It immediately strikes him as messy; more than messy, it is the kitchen of a person for whom the need to keep up appearances has gone. This kitchen is the way it is because it is easiest that way. Why clear things away when the next day they will come out again? Why tidy when it will just become messy again? He will learn over the coming months to wash his cups before he drinks, to remove the dust or the stains of the previous contents. As a prisoner, he does not have the privilege of being messy. He is just beginning to realise the journey he has to travel, the road along which he must go, back to the world that most people take for granted.

'How do you have your coffee? Black or white?'

'White, three sugars.'

He watches her wince at these words.

'Three sugars! How can you have that many?' she asks, not really expecting an answer – so when she gets one, it goes unheard.

'That's how I have always had it.'

She rummages in the cupboard for a while and eventually finds the sugar. She deliberately only puts in two sugars and hands it to him, then motions him to the table. He notices two tiny bits of what looks like hay floating in his drink. When seated, she starts a brief monologue, and as he listens he realises that this woman is like him. She, too, is nervous. She, too, is stiff and awkward with the conventions of conversation. This speech is the stitching together of all her random thoughts over the past few weeks.

'I haven't had one of your sort before. So it's new for me as much as you. Have you done a placement before? Anyway, I'm not getting any younger and there are some things I just can't do any more. I need somebody to help with the work on the farm. The hard work. The stuff that needs muscles. Each week, we can find a task on the Saturday that makes the farm work. I have sheep, you see, about sixty ewes. Lambing season is just beginning and I just feel permanently knackered, so I need your help.

'Today, I need your help fixing a gatepost that has sagged and to put some hard-core down to reduce the mud in a gateway.'

As they drink their coffee, the prisoner tries to make small talk.

'What are the dogs called?'

'Queenie is my old sheepdog,' Joyce begins, stroking the dog's head, almost without thinking. 'She is an old girl. After a life as a proper working sheepdog, she is now in semi-retirement with me.

The smaller flock and my neat parcels of fields, rather than the open fell, make for an easier life for her. I am afraid that, bit by bit, I have got softer and she has moved from the outdoor kennel to a bed by the Aga. She's an old lady like me, so I don't work her too hard. I'm not very good with my commands.'

'We do our best, don't we, Queenie,' she says, looking at the two dogs intently. She feeds each dog a biscuit and looks on affectionately as they wolf them down.

Steve imagines she probably talks like this to the dogs even if there is nobody else around.

'And this is Kipper. He is a mongrel from the rescue centre. Together they help me with my chores. They do like an extra morsel to keep them going. And they are what keep me going.'

They finish their coffee. Steve stands up and despite his uncertainty at what he is letting himself in for, tries to sound keen.

'Let's get to work on that gate.'

Out in the yard she shows him the tools and he piles them up into the wheelbarrow. He follows her across the yard towards the field nearest the sheep shed. He sees the problem at once. One of the gates into the field is sagging down, dragging in the thick sticky mud like a wounded leg on a battlefield. He watches her pull the gate open and sees the effort it takes this small figure with her gnarled lumpy hands to open the gates.

He watches as, with each step, her boots stick in the mud from the February rain. He watches as she drags and pauses and drags and pauses and he is filled with the seeds of admiration and sorrow. Admiration for the courage and toughness that this woman is showing and sorrow that there is no one to help her with this kind of work. Sorrow that she is all alone. He realises that he feels this sorrow because he feels for her, because he can see her loneliness – because, although her life is about as different from his as he can imagine, he can sense the strands that join them together.

Over the next two hours they fix the gate. He lifts it off its hinges and sends her off to find a spanner so that he can adjust the height. She returns with one that probably was last used before he was in prison. But in ten minutes he has lifted the gate. He has mended the wounded leg. He asks her how often she uses the gate, and she says four or five times a day.

And he has fixed it. He has saved her hours of dragging. She then shows him a pile of stone chippings and he takes five wheelbarrows' loads back to the gate and bit by bit he covers the mud and fills the holes. Finally, when the shepherdess says there are enough chippings, he smooths it down with a thumper. In two hours he has done a job that has made a difference.

Years from now he will look at this gateway, when he lives here with his own children, when he is the farmer, and this gateway will still for him be the place where it all began. Like a spot where a first girlfriend is kissed, this gate will become a marker, a milepost, for when his life began to change.

Once the job is finished they go in for lunch together. Again, this is all part of what the prison authorities request: that prisoners 'socialise' with their hosts to help them re-adjust to the outside world. It is then she asks him the question he dreads. The question he knew would be coming, although this makes it no easier. She asks him the question for which he has prepared his sanitised, role-playing, 'talking to the psychologist' answer. The prison tells him that part of the rehabilitation process is to answer his question. For him, now outside of the prison world, it would have been easier if she had asked about the size of his penis.

'What did you do?'

In that moment, a small crack opens in his carefully prepared world and he falls through. He tells her not what happened but how he feels.

'I killed, I murdered...' he says that last word slowly as his throat tightens, 'two people.'

As he continues, he chokes. His voice just seizes up, the phrases coming out with longer and longer pauses. 'I killed my...I can still hear, still hear...I can hear her when the nights are long and still, and I can't sleep. I can still hear them...I can still see their faces.'

He pauses. He is close to tears. His voice is choked. In all the sessions with the prison psychologists, he has never choked. But now, in front of a 'real' person, a person who could be his own mother, he chokes.

He looks up and he sees that she is looking at him. She had asked the question thinking that the answer would be simple. But she can see this is not going to be easy for him or for her. There they pause; there they stop for a moment in the raw, naked, terrible pain of a prisoner's remorse and a lonely woman's sympathy.

'Steve – not today, not today. Let's talk about this next time. I know we have to do this, that you have to tell me, but not today.'

His own reaction has surprised, even shocked him. For the prisoner, the journey back to normality is far from complete.

5: Running

Sunday 21st February

It is one of the last days of winter, where the patches of sun are chased up the fell by the hunting clouds: a sunlight fox with the cloud horses and hounds in hot pursuit. The old mine road slices up the Coledale valley below, and half way along, a solitary figure runs. Circling close, it's a tall, willowy figure pounding his way up the valley. His wild, tight-curled hair is barely contained by a hat. His legs are naked in the cold and on his pounding feet are new trainers, now dirtied by the mud of the February storms.

His hot breath comes out and mingles with the winter air. The cold winter sun is at his front and he is pushing himself to his limits. And first glance he looks a man, but as he draws closer, it is clear that it is a boy on the cusp of manhood. It is the same boy last seen on his final day at school way down south in Spitalfields. This is his first Sunday morning in the Lakes, and when he woke and looked out of his window he had the urge to run. He had the urge to be up in the hills: an urge like eating or sex or sleep that he cannot explain. He just wants to run.

His mother and sister are amazed, for he has never run before, at least not like this. Run for the bus, run in PE lessons (but only just), run in a game of football down at the park, but run for pleasure – never. He just put on the trainers bought for his first week at a new school, and now here he is.

And, although he is sweating and his fingers are cold, he is relishing it. So up the mine road he goes, up past the dead bracken of winter, past the Herdwicks that dot the fellside, past the beck that rushes down the valley as he rushes up. At the mine, he stops to catch his breath and looks at the old workings, and then down the slope and towards the place where the path crosses the beck. He tries to take the water in one stride, and his foot crashes into the stream but he doesn't stop. His legs keep going and now he begins the harder ascent, watching every step on the rocky path. Half way up, he pauses again. He turns to see from where he has come. The valley is below him and he is lost. Luckily, there is no one else here to see a moody teenager lost in awe at the meandering beck and the valley and the vast Skiddaw beyond. He cannot and could never describe what he is feeling, but the run, the hillside, the view below him have started an itch of feelings that he has never had before.

He turns to run again. He cuts across a path, heads for the skyline and the neck of the dip between Sail and Scar Crags. There is not really a proper path, so he is as much scrambling as running. He uses his hands now to clamber up the steep parts of his climb. He curses himself for not bringing a water bottle but then cups his hands to drink from a small stream that spouts over a rock. The coldness of the water makes him wince and he can feel the cold blood hit his head.

At the pass, he comes into sight of the Newlands Valley below, with Catbells in the distance. He can see the sun and the clouds over Robinson and Maiden Moor. And with fingers aching, lungs hurting, feet sore, legs cold, nose dripping, he realises he has never felt so much before. Every sense, every part of his body is talking to him and he in turn is trying to absorb the pain and the pleasure that come at him together.

He begins the descent into the valley below. The parts of his body that once were silent going uphill, are now talking. His toes push again and again in the front of his shoes. His knees and thighs ache with the strain of slowing his descent. He slithers down the road and pauses again. He still wants to run more, so he heads up the valley and towards the hills again.

He is running on tarmac now, in the narrow road that goes from Rolling Edge to Newtown. His legs are steadier on the flatter surface and he picks up the pace. He is surrounded by sheep fields on either side. Though he may not know it, lambing is yet to start in earnest. A few early daffodils pepper the roadside. He sees just a flash of white in the corner of his eye. He runs on. But then, as his brain brings all senses together, he stops. He stops and turns back. From the opposite direction, the flash of white is more obvious; it is a lamb wedged in the hedge. He edges closer and sees that the lamb is very small, very new and very cold. As he gets within a few feet it barely has the energy to move. It lets out a tiny noise. He can see that the lamb is all but gone. He reaches over the sheep netting and barbed wire and lifts the lamb up with one hand. With the other, he pulls back the bare twigs of the hedge and the lamb is in his arms. Still it barely struggles.

Now he is stuck. He has never held a lamb before, but he can see that it is cold and so he shoves it inside his fleece to keep it warm while he thinks. He looks up to see whose lamb it could be. He can see a farm entrance on the other side of the road and so he jogs down the drive to the farmhouse. The lamb is barely moving inside his fleece. He is worried it is dead as he holds the body up with one arm while knocking on the door with the other.

The woman who opens the door is used to the sight of tourists in the area. They have their own bed and breakfast guests. She is used to visitors who are overdressed or covered in mud from biking, or have the newest and best walking gear. But when she opens the door she sees a boy who for a cold February day is underdressed. His hair is a shocking mass of curls and tucked under a hat. His legs are muscular but bare. His shoes filthy and his fingers look freezing. He looks like a traveller from another land.

'Hello, young man,' she says in greeting.

'I found this lamb in the hedge,' he mumbles. 'I think it must be yours.'

'Let me see. Take it out from under that fleece. He looks snug in there. He must be cold – aye, he is, but he's not one of ours. He's the wrong colour. His nose is too black for one of our flock. Our lambs are black from the Herdwicks, or have black feet if they are Swaledale. He must belong to the southern lady, the Suffolk shepherdess.'

He can barely understand her accent.

'The shepherdess,' he repeats, sounding like a foreign tourist who has just picked up a single word of French from a whole conversation.

'Aye, lad. Shepherdess is just up the road. Come out of our drive and turn left, walk about 200 yards and you'll see her farm on the other side. It's called Newtown Turn Farm – there's a sign.'

'Thank you,' he says, relieved that she gestured with her directions.

'No bother,' she replies, and shuts the door behind him.

He sets off down the drive and jogs gently up the road till he finds the sign for Newtown Turn Farm. He is not quite sure what to expect of the shepherdess. The tone in the woman's voice made the shepherdess sound a little like a stranger to her – a foreigner in this land, like him.

He knocks on the door and there is no answer. It is a slate farmhouse in a small courtyard, with a barn on one side of the square, and a shed with a rusting tractor in it on the other side. He knocks again. The next thing he knows, there are two dogs sniffing his feet. As soon as they catch the smell of lamb, they sniff towards his fleece. The lamb still does not move.

Moments later, the shepherdess appears from round the corner. Her face is ruddy from the sun and wind at the end of a cold winter. She greets him with barely a pause for breath.

'Hello, I thought I heard someone. What can I do for you?'

'Well...I found a lamb in the hedge. I think it's very cold.'

'Oh!' the shepherdess says. She pauses then says, 'You had better come inside the house then.'

They enter her huge kitchen. He has never seen one like it. He is used to his mother's small, neat kitchen with its clean chipboard units. This one has an Aga and, despite the sunshine, it is dark in the low winter light.

'Now let me see, who have we got here?'

He hands her the lamb. It is still more dead than alive. She takes it carefully.

'Yes, it is one of mine, and it is very cold. We need to warm it up. Hold it again.'

And with this, she hands the lamb back, and then goes to the larder in the corner of the room and after a few moments rummaging she reappears as a hobbit might reappear from its lair with a trophy.

'This is what we need. A spell in the oven will help it.'

She shows him a squat cardboard box, and then takes the lamb, places it inside, and closes the lid. He looks at her as if he has suddenly fallen down the rabbit hole in *Alice in Wonderland*.

'The oven – what do you mean?' he blurts.

'The oven is what a lamb needs.'

She puts the cardboard box in the bottom oven of the stove.

'You can't cook it alive!' he all but shouts at her.

She turns round calmly.

'I am not cooking it at all. The lamb is cold. If we don't warm it up, it will die. This is just the warming drawer. Short of giving the lamb a warm bath, this is the next best thing. Twenty minutes from now, the lamb will either have not recovered or will be dancing round my kitchen and desperate for a feed. So we had better go and see if we can find the lamb's mother. Follow me.'

Leaving the lamb in the Aga, she marches out of the kitchen and into the yard, grabbing her coat on the way. He is still stunned by what he has just seen, but, unable to resist her flow, he follows.

She strides out across the yard. They cross into the field and he realises that it is the same field where he found the lamb, but from the inside. Now he has stopped running, he is beginning to get cold and wishes this woman had offered him a coat. But she doesn't.

In the field are about fifty ewes. Some are heavy with lamb, a few are grazing as their new offspring huddle together in the sunshine trying to keep out of the wind. The lambs are different sizes. There is one lamb he notices about three times the size of the rest. One set of twins is brand new and he can see the ewe licking them clean, her afterbirth dangling from her uterus. In between are lambs that are now scampering and jumping.

In the field the shepherdess stops.

'We need to see if we can find a ewe that is missing a lamb. If we can't re-unite the lamb with its mother soon, she will reject it even if it is hers. Once a ewe rejects a lamb, it's very hard to overcome,' she tells him. She pauses while she searches and continues, 'I have skinned dead lambs to try and persuade a ewe to adopt another lamb. You tie the coat of the dead lamb to the abandoned one so that it smells right. It rarely works, though, as the ewe still rejects the lamb.'

She is almost talking to herself.

'You can smear a lamb with the afterbirth so the ewe never knows she lost a lamb. But that only works if the lamb dies at birth. I have kept a ewe penned, head tied, with a lamb that needs adopting. Then it's my will versus the ewe's. I have seen ewes kill a lamb that wasn't theirs. But normally, out in the field, the lamb just gets thinner and thinner as it starves. I must check my records.'

But she never does.

The fell-runner doesn't yet know it but over the next few months he will get to know the full wonder of the shepherdess's habits and lifestyle. He will share more of his secrets with her than with any person he has ever met before. She will tell him more of her past than she has told anyone. The prisoner will be whom she occasionally refers to as her 'Saturday man' and the fell-runner her 'Sunday boy'.

They search the field and can see no ewe missing a lamb. They return to the farmhouse.

She marches straight to the Aga and pulls out the box and puts it on the floor. The lamb stands almost straightaway. He cannot believe the difference. Twenty minutes ago it was half dead and now it stands tottering on the flagstone floor, uncertain where to turn.

'We must feed it. It will have to stay in the kitchen until I can foster it. I just need to make up some milk for it. Would you like to feed it?'

She returns to the larder and pulls out a plastic bucket with white powder in it. She puts two scoops in a plastic jug and half

37

boils the kettle, and then mixes up the jug to the top. She then pours the frothy white liquid into a bottle she has dug out of a cupboard. She reaches into a drawer and screws on a rubber teat. He watches, fascinated.

He remembers this day, this moment in particular, as he sits by her hospital bed, years later, as she sleeps. He remembers that this was the perfect introduction to the shepherdess. It summed her up in every way: practical, caring, brusque, and eccentric. When the bottle is finally ready, she tilts it and drizzles some on the back of her hand. The ritual of preparing the milk and feeding the lamb is so well polished it happens in a few moments. By that same hospital bed, he remembers that when he tried to do the same thing a few days later, it took half an hour. The milk was too hot and too lumpy. The teat got constantly clogged and the desperate lamb frustrated. Her smooth expertise made it look easy.

She offers him the bottle. He looks at it, horrified.

'You found it,' she says. 'It lives because of you. You should learn to feed it. Take the bottle and hold the lamb with the other hand. Now show it the teat. It will have no idea what to do at first. Don't let it get away. Put one hand under the tummy. Squirt some milk onto the teat and hold his mouth with a thumb. That's how it gets the teat in its mouth so it can taste the milk. Now squirt a little milk down its throat.'

He wants another hand. He has never felt so clumsy, but gradually, the lamb gets the idea. He removes the hand from its tummy as now it wants to feed. Soon it is pushing hard at the teat wanting more milk. It takes about a third of the bottle and stops.

'That will do for now,' she says. 'Otherwise, it will drink too much. Lambs have been known to drink themselves to death. In the field they can never get enough milk, so if they drink artificial milk, they have nothing that tells them to stop.

'So you've fed a lamb now. How did it feel?'

It is not a good combination for a balanced conversation. The shy awkward teenager and the elderly woman who doesn't have anyone for company and, after many years of living alone, has simply forgotten the norms of social intercourse.

'Good.'

'Well, you have made a new friend now, one that will need feeding three times a day. Are you local, by the way?' she asks bluntly, then adds, 'You don't look local!'

'I've just moved to Portinscale.'

'Well, please do come back and help with the lamb. Thank you for all your help today.'

He moves to the door.

'I might well do that. I must get back to my run now.'

'Of course, you must.' There is an awkward pause, almost as if she is trying to work out how to prolong the conversation.

'Would you like to give the lamb a name? Bottle-fed lambs need names.'

He pauses, taken back by this offer.

'Jessica,' he says, after a long gap. 'I'd like to call it Jessica, after my mum.'

'Very well. Jessica it is.'

And with that, he shuts the farmhouse door and sets off, heading back along the farm track to finish his now highly delayed run. She forgets to tell him the lamb is male.

6: A new school

Monday 22nd February

The lamb-rescuing fell-runner is on his first day at his new school in Keswick. His new school in a small town in the centre of the Lakes feels a long way from his old school in the centre of a huge city to the first day.

He has joined the sixth form, halfway through the first year. It's not a good time to join. Friendships are already made, alliances forged, classroom seats agreed. The dust is settled on the ecology of friendships. And he has to decide whether to disturb some of that dust, whether to prise his way into the friendship groups that already exist.

Today is not the day for that, as this is his first day. He is determined to be detached, to be noticed, but not too keen, not too engaged. In his mind, the rush of pupils around him during the school day will leave him like a boulder in the stream.

To the pupils, he is the new boy. Today, they are the chattering classes. They are the excited puppies to his haughty adult. They see a tall skinny boy with wild unkempt hair. They see a boy who walks differently from them, who talks differently from them, who oozes the coolness of the city, making them feel like country bumpkins.

He finds his way to his first lesson with the help of his buddy, assigned to him by the school. He is called Graham, and if the school had seen them both together they would never have paired them up. While the newcomer is now over six foot, Graham is nearly six inches shorter. While the newcomer has presence, Graham constantly fiddles with his clothes and adjusts his spectacles. Graham meets him outside the school secretary's office and takes him to the classroom where the teacher introduces him.

'Class, we have a new pupil who has joined the school. His name is Ashley Smith. Ashley, would you like to tell us about yourself?'

Ashley pauses and then stands.

'Hi, everyone. My name is Ashley. I have just moved up from London. My mum has got a job here. I am doing history, geography, biology and ICT for AS levels. I used to go to school in the east side of London in a place called Spitalfields.'

His first lesson is Geography. In his mind, he is walking slowly, measured, distanced. His mother has dragged him up here, and even though he knows why, he is determined not to settle in easily.

But his outer calm is not matched on the inside because in Geography he is sitting next to a girl. She is tall – nearly as tall as him, he notices.

'Hey,' she says as they sit down.

'Hey,' he replies, although he is now finding it hard to be cool and aloof. It's easy with a whole class, but a single girl is a different matter.

For she is not just tall, she is willowy, with a good figure and handsome face and high cheekbones. She, moves with poise and confidence.

As the lesson progresses, she answers the question that the teacher poses. She makes notes. She is attentive. He is used to classes where getting pupils to be attentive, to be keen, is impossible. Disinterested and diffident is what every boy, except the geeks, wants to be. Not that this girl could ever be called a geek; she is far too alluring for that.

When the teacher asks him a question, he has not been listening. He asks the teacher to repeat herself, and still he cannot answer. He is relieved when the lesson is over. She turns to him as the lesson ends and smiles.

'You didn't take any notes. Do you remember it all in your head?'

He is not sure how to take this. Is she flirting, or teasing, or just a geek in warrior princess clothing?

'I remember it all in my head, of course.'

'I didn't catch your name.'

'Ashley,' he replies, and can think of nothing to add.

He has already turned his back, so he cannot see her pulling a face at his back as she adds, 'And mine is Jess.'

If the fell-runner had wanted to create the impression of being aloof and enigmatic in his first few days at school, he has done so. While his classmates can see that he is different, they find all their attempts at friendliness rebuffed. He answers questions with monosyllabic answers.

On the inside the fell-runner is not indifferent. The girl from the Geography class turns out to be doing three of the same four subjects as him. After two weeks, he has moved from indifference to infatuation. He has stared at her in class, watched her talk with friends in the playground, and seen her walking home from school.

Sadly, all she sees is the new boy who she thinks is an arsehole and, unlike any other boy she has met, has rebuffed her friendliness. She is used to being the centre of boys' attention, not their indifference. Only the passing of time will show if this changes.

At home, his mum asks him how the new school is going. She is keen to know. Her guilt at the uprooting of her two children is acute. Although to the outside world she and her daughter are closer, he is her baby, her first-born, her boy. But the relationship between mother and son, so rich and so rewarding before teenage years, is now strained. His hormones are surging round his body. His body is growing in a thousand ways and places: pubes, armpit hair, spots, breaking voice, and the first sign of stubble. And on the inside there are even more changes, as he struggles to work out who he is and where he fits in.

So the beamish boy of primary school has become the monosyllabic oaf of teenage years. He grunts and lies on the sofa, prone to watching telly for hours or becoming completely absorbed on his PlayStation. Like so many mothers, she yearns for the child she knew. He has grown not from caterpillar into beautiful butterfly, but from butterfly into silent caterpillar. Like the parents of most teenagers, she hopes he will grow back into a butterfly again.

But a mother's love doesn't stop just because the child changes. Like a boat in stormy seas, she still wants to reach calmer emotional waters. She has left London to start again, to escape the man who made life unbearable. But she knows that her children, especially Ashley, were traumatised by what they saw, by what the man they called 'dad' did to her. She knows they have been deeply affected by the move which has uprooted them from friends, from family, and from the streets of east London they knew so well.

She wants reassurance that she has done the right thing. She is desperate to know that school is going well. This is not a pleasure that Ashley is prepared to give her. The reality is that he has no idea what he thinks. How does he judge a new school? He is not trying to make new friends. There are a few boys who he grunts a greeting to, and with whom he plays football at lunchtime. He is not going to tell his mother in a million years that there is a girl, another Jessica – or, as she usually calls herself, Jess – the girl he sat next to in his first lessons and it is she who absorbs his thoughts.

In fact, she has guessed that something is happening. She notices things that only a mother can. He has started to go running. He is gone for hours, and says he is just running. And she notices the more subtle things: the appearance of deodorant and aftershave in his bedroom. The extra time he spends in front of the mirror since they moved. And, above all, she notices that he has brushed his hair. He has always had a great knotted tangle of hair; frizzy and unkempt, wild and long. His behaviour has all the hallmarks of a crush, behaviour she well recognises from her own teenage years.

She catches him one morning brushing his hair, standing at his bedroom door. He stands with his back to her.

'Toto,' she calls softly, and pauses, using a nickname she has used since he was a baby. 'Toto, your hair looks nice when you brush it. Any particular reason?'

'No reason,' he says without catching her eyes, 'just removing a tangle.' But he hasn't brushed his hair voluntarily since he was twelve.

He has never cared about how he looks. So if something, or more accurately someone, is making him brush his hair, school can't be all bad.

7: Music after birth

Sunday 28th March

There are sheep everywhere. Ewes about to give birth, or who have given birth an hour or a day ago. Lambs just born, that are discovering their legs, that are hungry. Perhaps their mother has infected teats full of mastitis, or their older sibling is beating them to the milk or they were rejected at birth.

There are ewes that are struggling to give birth and for some, despite hours of pushing, no lamb is born. There may be nothing to show for it – or just a foot or a mouth with a blue tongue poking out. These ewes need the shepherd or even the vet to help them. Without that help, the ewe or her lambs will probably die. A shepherdess has to be everywhere, all the time.

Underfoot is straw, mixed with sodden hay. The shepherdess should change the bedding, put down new straw, but there isn't time. And the ewes need feeding with hay and sheep nuts – pellets of concentrated high energy food. They need checking, and once they have been checked, they need checking again a few hours later. There are a few hours when a ewe in labour or a lamb in distress can be saved. And whatever time that is, day or night, the shepherdess needs to be there to save lives.

The shepherdess's day at lambing time begins at 6 a.m. when all the ewes are checked. Any ewe about to lamb is put in a separate pen. The dogs follow at her heels, looking for a snack of some afterbirth, or some loose sheep nuts. The shepherdess looks for lambs who are not thriving, who might need extra milk from their ewe, and she will then pin the angry ewe against the side of the pen while the lamb feeds. By 8 a.m., she is desperate for a cup of tea, but the ewes and the lambs come first.

Each lamb that is born and each ewe that gives birth must be checked. Does the ewe have milk? Has the lamb started to breathe? Has it suckled? Is the mother accepting her lambs? Has the umbilical cord been sprayed with iodine? Has the placenta come away? Or is there another lamb inside?

And then the hardest job of all – checking the sheep in the middle of the night. The alarm may go off at 3 a.m. Every ounce of her body just wants to turn over and go back to sleep, to stay in her warm bed, but she knows that if she goes back to sleep, the golden hours for a lamb may be gone, or a ewe may have prolapsed and pushed her insides out. A lamb may be dead if the sheep are not checked. And so the shepherdess, half-asleep, dresses, desperately hoping, that no ewe will be in labour, that no job will need to be done. That no lamb will need help and that the warm bed will soon be welcoming her back.

And when an hour or two later she does return to the house, experience tells her that the deep sleep of a comfy bed is harder to wake from than dozing on the sofa. And at 6 a.m. the alarm will go off and the whole cycle begins again.

The fell-runner has taken to spending his Sunday afternoons down with the shepherdess on the farm to help out with the sheep. He runs from the house in Portinscale and then up the Newlands Valley or, if he is feeling energetic, up the Catbells

Terrace and onto Maiden Moor and down the steep fell to her farm.

Today he runs straight there. He wants to see his lamb. He wants to see it guzzle a bottle and run to him with delight. Ashley is growing used to the eccentricity of the old shepherdess and he feels useful when he is at the farm.

As soon as he enters the farmyard, she greets him and says he must come to help with a lambing. A ewe is in a pen and is straining. Her black head twists up and sideways. Her body ripples with a contraction and then relaxes. He has never seen this before, but he has no time to watch or wonder. The shepherdess is thrusting towels and an empty bucket at him, while telling him the ewe is taking too long.

'We need water in the bucket, and she needs her head tied to the side of the pen – or you can hold her,' she tells him.

Ashley, a city boy, is used to buses and tubes, congestion and buildings, and now he is helping lambs come into the world. As his mind whirls, he notices Jessica, desperate Jessica, pacing back and forth by the side of the pen nearest his feet. He hears her bleat, her hungry bleat, and his heart melts.

Jessica has to wait for her feed as Joyce is insistent that he helps. She almost pushes him into the pen.

'Take her head and pull her to the side,' Joyce tells him. 'Now tie her by the neck using the rope to the side of the pen.'

He tries, but the ewe can still move.

'Hold her head then and talk to her. I need to investigate what is wrong.'

The shepherdess kneels down and her bottom lip is pulled taut in concentration as she cups her hand and eases it inside the ewe. He is almost sick. She has covered her hand in gel and she pushes it further inside.

'Ah,' she cries, almost as much to herself as to him. 'The lamb has one front leg back. We just need to ease it round. I need to push the head back gently and create space to move the front leg forward. You see for a lamb to come out the two front legs and the nose must all point together, but if one leg is back the shoulder sticks out and gets stuck. So I am pushing the head back and we have got the leg round.'

She looks up momentarily and notices that the fell-runner is standing motionless and glass-eyed, holding the ewe's head.

'Are you all right?' she asks. He doesn't answer.

He is not all right. He feels like he is about to be throw up. His mum may be a nurse, but he has never seen this before. He has seen kids shooting up at school, kickings in the playground, knife attacks on the street, but now a woman and a ewe are making him queasy. He has never watched a birth. He has never seen an elderly lady put her hand inside a sheep and pull the lamb around. And he feels ill.

He is just about to reply when the first lamb tumbles out. Joyce smiles as the lamb kicks and struggles. She quickly puts her hand back inside the ewe and then quickly pulls it out again.

'Fantastic.'

The second lamb should come out without a hitch.

'Can I leave you here to watch them and make sure the second lamb is OK? I need to get on with feeding the ewes outside. Oh, and it looks like Jessica needs a feed too.'

She gesticulates at the still-desperate Jessica, who is pacing the rails of her pen. Ashley nods in agreement, pleased to be left alone. He puts his earphones back in and withdraws into his world as he fills the bottle for Jessica from the jug of formula milk that Joyce has prepared.

Jessica is ravenous, greedy. Her head goes through the bar

to reach for the teat of the feeding bottle. She drinks as fast as she can. Joyce has told him to make sure that she doesn't drink too fast, so he pulls the teat back just a little and watches the air bubbles shoot in. With the headphones on, he switches off to the outside world.

Soon she has drunk three-quarters of the bottle. His thoughts wander. He loves the way Jessica makes him feel. Nothing has ever made him feel as wanted as she does. He knows that she exists because of him; another few hours, and she would have died in the cold wind back in February. Imagining her stiff, cold lifeless body chokes him up, but here she is, feeding from his bottle. He has given her life. He has given her food. She recognises him. She knows his voice, even though she doesn't see him every day.

He then suddenly remembers that he is meant to be looking out for the second lamb. He stands up from the hay bale where he has been feeding Jessica and goes over to see if the second lamb has been born.

What he sees makes him gasp. He walks towards the pen to get a better look. There are two lambs. But there is mucus, there is blood, there is a huge pile of what looks like the bloody inside of a sheep. It seems to him that her intestines, her uterus, her everything are coming out. He panics. Though the ewe seems all right her insides are coming out. And then from nowhere he leans over and vomits uncontrollably onto the straw.

Though there is no one in the shed but him, he is embarrassed. Embarrassed that big, tough, aloof Ashley has seen the inside of a sheep and vomited. He finds a pile of straw and covers up his sick. He certainly doesn't want Joyce to see it. He then leaves the sheep shed to find her, so that he can tell her to call the vet. He is convinced that the ewe, whose head he has just held, is dying.

A minute or so later, they return to the shed as he tells her about the intestines, the insides he has just seen. She is panicked and her face shows it, but as they reach the pen, her face changes.

She sits on a hay bale by the pen and begins to chuckle. Her anxiety has turned into amusement. He looks at her with amazement. How can she laugh when her ewe is dying? His face turns from amazed to quizzical to angry.

'Why are you laughing? How can you laugh when she is dying?'

'She isn't dying,' she says, looking at him. 'That's her afterbirth, her placenta. That's where the lambs were connected to her.'

She can see it in his face as the penny drops. 'I thought you studied biology at school.'

'I do,' he replies, and he begins to laugh as well. Laughing out of relief, laughing to hide the humiliation, laughing to convert all that emotional energy into another form. As they laugh, the dogs catch a whiff of his vomit and begin to sniff near it. He suddenly realises what they are doing. As he laughs his foot pushes a little more straw over his sick without it being obvious what he is up to. The dogs persist at the smell. As they talk he tries to push the dogs away with his foot. In desperation he stands on top of the straw he has just pushed over his sick.

'Now I know the ewe is all right, let's clear up in here and then go and get a cup of tea and bit of a cake. It's getting dark. First of all, let me show you what to do with newborn lambs.

'Are those dogs all right? They seem very interested in whatever you are standing on.'

'Really?' he replies, feigning surprise. 'I hadn't noticed.'

He catches just the faintest curl of a suppressed smile at the corners of Joyce's mother and can't decide if she has guessed what is going on. She says nothing more.

While the ewe nuzzles and chunners over her new-born lambs, Joyce shows him what needs to be done after lambs are born. She shows him how to rub the lambs down with straw to get rid of the mucus and meconium. She makes him put the afterbirth in the bin, telling him how the dogs love to eat it and for a split second he thinks he might be sick again. She shows him how to make sure that the lambs know where the ewe's teats are. He fetches the ewe some fresh water and she tells him to tie the bucket to the rail to stop it falling over.

Inside, she makes them both a cup of tea. They sit down and she offers him a slice of lemon drizzle cake. He accepts.

'Well, I might make a sheep farmer of you yet. There are so many things that need to be remembered, but you did well today. The ewe had two lambs. They both came out alive, and I'd always rather that people were over-cautious if they thought something was wrong than say nothing. What were you doing when I left? Were you watching the ewe?'

'Well, ah, well, no, I was feeding Jessica so I got a bit distracted and I had my headphones on.'

'Well that explains it all. You had gone off into another world. I want to find out what is on those headphones that you like to listen to so much and that distract you so much. What were you listening to?'

'Music,' he replies, not sure he likes where the conversation is heading.

'I realise music! But who? Anybody I would have heard of?'

'I very much doubt it. She's called Sinead O'Connor. My mum likes her.'

'Is she one of those modern musicians? What is it called, "the hop-hip music"?'

'Hip-hop, not hop-hip. How do you know about that? No, she just sings really, sings beautifully.'

'Can I listen?'

'Only if I can hear what you'd listen to on your headphones – if you had any.'

'Well, that serves me right. What would I listen to on my headphones? Well, I can do better than that. I will play you the music I listen to. Do you know Verdi's *La Traviata*? It's a love story. Follow me.'

In the living room she pulls up two armchairs next to each other and in front of her hi-fi. They sit in the half-light of her living room.

'I am afraid I don't have CDs, just a gramophone. So this is *La Traviata*. This is the last scene. There are two people called Alfredo and Violetta and they are in love with each other. But like so many lovers, they are being proud, being vain, being aloof, and not admitting to each other that they are in love. They are from two different social backgrounds. The story is from a time when love like that was not so easy. She is from a poor background and has climbed her way up the social ladder. He is an intellectual, a writer, I think. So he goes away, because they can't get it together.

'Now he is returning. He has heard that she is dying from consumption, from TB. She is in her bedroom when her maid rushes in to tell her that Alfredo has returned. She perks up. But she is ill. She is dying. So at last they declare their love for each other. They talk about going to live in the country, about leaving the city. They sing to each other of their future together. As she rises to try and dress herself she falls back, exhausted. They call for the doctor but it is too late. She is dying and he tells her they will be together forever. She slumps back and dies.

'It is tragic. It is love at its most heart-wrenching. Verdi knew how to write these stories. Just listen to the emotion.'

She puts the needle on the record and sits down. The old vinyl record crackles.

He hears these two voices. He listens in the half-darkness. It is music that he would never listen to. But he can hear the love as they sing. He thinks about what she has said about lovers being aloof and not getting it together in time. Leaping forward in his imagination, he pictures the scene not as Alfredo and Violetta, but as Ashley and Jess the object of his infatuation. This is his fantasy and daydream. As a result, as he listens he is moved. He will not admit it. He steals a glance at her. She has her eyes closed, soaking in the music until there is silence.

'Now it's your turn. What are we going to listen to?'

'This is,' he says, 'this is Sinead O'Connor, her song "Nothing compares to you". It's her singing about a relationship that has ended. She starts by singing about all the good things about not being in a relationship. She can go to fancy restaurants. She can get up and go to bed when she likes. Then she cracks and admits that none of this makes up for her loss, that "nothing compares to you". Somebody told me that her mother died not long before this song was written, and so the pain in this song is about her double loss. I am afraid you will have to listen to it on my headphones.'

He puts one headphone in her ear, and moving their chairs closer, he puts one in his ear.

She sits listening. She hears a pure strong voice. She hears a voice that is soaked in pain and emotion. She listens to the words and thinks of herself and the husband she left behind, the man whose life she ripped apart. She wonders if this is what he sang as he grieved about her departure. She thinks about the pain of her past and the pain of their separation. Even though she knows she was right, she believes she was right, she feels for the man she left and what he must have felt. She hasn't ever felt this before. She hasn't thought about him or his feelings in years. All she knows is that her children have never really forgiven her. As the music finishes, it is her turn to steal a glance. It is his turn for eyes to be closed but, as she turns her head, the earphone falls out and his eyes are open in an instant.

'What did you think?' he asks.

'It was good,' she says. 'What did you think about Alfredo and Violetta?'

'It was okay,' he says.

Neither of them is really prepared to admit that the other's music has moved them, but inside both of them, even though neither of them yet knows it, there is the smallest crack in the armour plating of their loneliness.

8: Talking and worming

Saturday 10th April

'Steve. Let's try again. What did you do?'

It sounds like an innocent question. When asked of a lifer out on day release, it is far from innocent. It is a question that he has dreaded since he started working with Joyce. She has let it lie for the last two months since she first asked. He knows that he must answer it. He knows this is part of what rehabilitation and repentance is all about. This is hard for both of them. Joyce is growing to like Steve. What if he reveals crimes which make her fearful or she finds repugnant? She doesn't want to find herself repulsed by his crimes and unable to have him visit her anymore.

They are not face to face, but out in the barn, worming the ewes and the young lambs. One by one slowly they have to squirt a dose of wormer into every the mouth of every ewe. As he moves between the ewes he begins his story slowly as if winded, as if forcing the words out between breaths.

'I killed two people. Two people I cared for.'

'Start at the beginning, Steve. What happened?' she says while grabbing the head of the next ewe. 'Hold her head. No, this way a little more.'

'I was nineteen. I was training to be an accountant and there was this girl working in a sandwich shop. She started to flirt with me when I got sandwiches at lunch and I was flattered.'

He pauses for breath 'So this girl, Kylie, and I, we started dating.'

For the first time, with nothing to prove, he is talking as much to himself as to her.

'It was a crazy time and in the midst of all that lust and not much love she got pregnant. It wasn't what either of us wanted. She wouldn't have an abortion. Her mother would go ape, she said. I said my mother would go ape. Besides, she said, it was the drudge of the sandwich shop or the baby. I was too young, too stupid, too weak, to stop her getting pregnant in the first place, and too weak to make her see how young we were.'

He glances up at Joyce to try and gauge her reaction, but her eyes are fixed firmly on the ewe.

'So, we had a baby. And once the baby was born two things began to happen, one wonderful and one terrible. The wonderful thing was the delight of falling in love with a baby. The joy, the wonder of bringing a small being into the world and bit by bit, piece by piece, smile by smile discovering what love is like.'

'And the terrible thing?'

'The terrible thing was Kylie began to change. She loved Zoe but it didn't transform her. It didn't change the way she saw the world in the way it did for me. For her Zoe was as much jailer as liberator. She was too young. We were both too young. Kylie began to resent what the baby had done to her freedom. But she didn't take it out on Zoe but on me.

'She told me how useless I was at changing nappies, at feeding her with a bottle, at everything. She took all her anger out on me. For the most part I just took her blows of anger like a punch bag.

Because you see the more she came to resent her situation, the more she took it out on me. She kept me as far from my baby as she could. She stopped me helping.

'But once in every few days I would manage to sneak a few moments alone with my daughter when her mother was on the loo or resting. And my daughter, my daughter, would look at me and smile. She would gurgle at me happily. I was in love. She was my daughter. But her mother would wake up or come back and again, in a moment, I went from the father who could make his daughter smile and gurgle to the useless husband. I was the man who had trapped her, the man who couldn't even change a nappy.'

'So, what went wrong?' Joyce passes another ewe out into the yard and motions to him to bring the next ewe along.

'I was angry. So angry. Angry that I wasn't at university.'

'Why didn't you go to uni?'

'My parents didn't want me to do. So they wouldn't support me. So I was angry about that. Angry about the tiny flat. Angry that was I was being kept from my gorgeous daughter. My mother had come to stay and she wound me up too. I was angry with everyone!

'So, I went out drinking after work with my mates one night. That was the first mistake.

'I got home and was ready to have it out my mother and Kylie. Ready to tell them both what I thought. But when I got through the door, it wasn't what I was expecting.'

'Why, what happened?'

'It was just her, just her.'

'Just who?'

He tries to speak, but emotion has overcome him. He hangs his head down. The tears drip down. They say nothing for a minute.

'I'm sorry, I can't go on. I have told you what I am required to do. I killed two people. I hope that is enough.'

He looks over at the shepherdess plaintively. 'You asked a straightforward question and I have given you a long emotional answer. In prison we get these sessions with the shrinks and we have to tell them just what they want to hear. Not too much, not too weird, not too conventional. We all learn the script. We learn to be in control of our feelings, about what we reveal. I have told no one what I felt in that room. I got a little further today. But because I pleaded guilty to everything, to two counts of murder, I have never had to tell anyone. Today I have opened a little more, but not enough. I can't do it. I'm sorry.'

'Don't be sorry at all. Sometimes these things need to be said. We all have things we need to say. I am happy to listen. I am happy to help,' she says.

Emotions are infectious. Had he been able to see Joyce's face, he would have seen her shining eyes and her pain as he has told his story. He would have seen that she has been no idle listener but attentive to his every word. Her pain and his have joined in her head as he talks. Her journey, how she has come to be standing in this yard, with these sheep, is not simple, but for the first time, she has felt humbled by somebody else's story. She need not have worried that his story would repulse her. Quite the opposite. For the first time in years, she has met and listened to a story that puts her emotional journey in the shadows. She has a growing feeling that he, too, is part of her flock, to be tended, nurtured, and supported.

'I hope you don't mind. I hope you mean that.'

'Has prison has been good for you, then? It has given you all that time to think, maybe even the university you never got.'

He laughs. 'I have never thought about prison in that way. Perhaps prison is good for my head, good for my learning. It has given me a lot of time to think. I have read every book I could get my hands on. I have sucked up all the learning I could but prison is a terrible, terrible place.'

'Terrible in what way – apart from the obvious, of course?'

He pauses a moment and then starts again. 'In my first prison, there was a bug room for new prisoners.' He tries to look at her again, to catch her eye.

'A bug room?' she repeats, without looking up from the ewe she is dosing.

'A bug room. New prisoners go in there. I went there on my first night. Everybody knows which cell it is. To begin with, you think the screws are being nice. You have a room to yourself on your first night. But every prisoner in the wing is waiting for the screams to start. For the prisoner to notice.'

'To notice what?' she asks, looking at him at last.

'To notice that this is a room where they harvest, where they grow bedbugs. Big fat bastards! If you are lucky, the last prisoner may have been in only a few days earlier. When I went in, it was a month. The bedbugs were ravenous.

'At first I didn't notice anything was wrong. I thought I was lucky to have a room of my own to settle into. I was pleased to have some privacy, to have the room, the blankets, and the pillows all to myself. There I was, listening to my music on my headphones and reading a magazine. Bliss. Then I turned over and noticed what looks like a walking apple pip marching up the blanket towards me. My eyes then tuned in, focusing on these 'things', and I saw half a dozen apple pips. All on the march.

'I had no idea what they were. You hear prisoners talking about so many bugs and parasites in prison, pubic crab lice, head lice, and the rest of the works. What I know now and discovered very quickly is that they were bed bugs; ravenous, bloodsucking bed bugs. They feast on blood. They start out as tiny pinpricks too small to see and then grow to the size of apple pips.

'Even if I didn't know what they were, I knew they weren't nice. I leapt off the bed. I squeezed all the ones I could see between my fingernails. I searched all the corners of the bed and killed all the ones I found. But their size meant I couldn't see them all. It was like some scene from *Star Wars*. Every time I thought I had killed all the little bastards another wave came marching out attracted by my body heat. They were remorseless. They hid in every nook and cranny of the bed and the bedding. They hid in the sewn over edges of the blanket and the insides of the mattress, in the dust-filled corners of the bed frame. They were there waiting for me.

'I shouted for the guard. This is the moment they had all been waiting for. Apparently they lay bets on how long each new prisoner will last before he calls for the guard. From across the cells there was a cheer. I lasted longer than most, apparently.

'The guard came over and I told him that there were bugs on my bed. He looked in and asked me what the fuss was all about. I told him that there were bugs on my bed. He opened the door and entered. He couldn't see anything, he told me. It slowly dawned on me that this was no accident. The barely suppressed grin on his face told me that something was afoot. This was all part of the game.

'And his parting words were "Good night – hope the bugs don't bite."

'In the night, I felt a thousand bugs crawling over me but when I turned on the light, they were all in my imagination. Eventually, I fell asleep and dreamt of bugs.

'In the morning I was covered in bites. My ankles were ringed with them. Along my legs there were lines of 'breakfast, lunch and dinner' bites, as the website I found later called them. They were round my neck, in my crotch, maybe 300 in all. I itched for days.

'And of course, then, I moved cells, and I was given a shower with an insect killer. They took away all my clothes and washed them. The screws made a point of coming to tell me in mock horror they had found bedbugs in my room.

'Every other prisoner knew I was the one in the bug room the previous night. They all tittered. A few told me their stories. It was the prison's way of making sure I knew my place, making sure I was humiliated.

'So when you say prison may have been good for me you could be right. Anybody who goes in a proud man, a man who walks tall, doesn't come out that way. For some that is what they need – to be forced to come to terms with their own fragility. For most prisoners that extraction of pride means that self-esteem, belief that they are a human being whose thoughts, feelings, desires, are of any importance, is all but gone.'

The shepherdess finally looks at him. Others would be more judgemental of him and his crimes. Others would be fearful for themselves. Others would think of Kylie and her family. Others would make sure they were never alone with a murderer. None of this occurs to Joyce. For in Steve she can see somebody who she can help. Who needs her. And in her loneliness needing to be needed is an emotion so powerful that any other responses are impossible. The shepherdess finally looks at him and smiles:

'When I decided to apply for a prisoner from Fellview on day release, I thought it would be good to help me with my jobs. I thought it would make sense for the muscle you would bring. I never imagined you would open my eyes to a world I had never really thought about.'

'And I never imagined I would know how to dose a sheep for parasites and trim their feet,' he responds, smiling.

9: Out with the dogs

Saturday 8th May

As spring reaches its peak in May and the days warm up, the long wool winter coats of a ewe need shearing. Joyce doesn't do any of her own shearing; instead, she pays two semi-retired shepherds, Ken and Derek. Her small flock of ewes is not a whole day's work, indeed for Ken and Derek's experienced hands it is barely a morning's work. The prisoner is here to help too. But because of her southern breeds the ewes are heavier than the usual breeds of Herdwicks and Swaledales in the area. They are harder work but the fleeces are bigger and of a better quality. Indeed, Joyce pays Ken and Derek with the fleeces of her flock.

As Ken and Derek shear the ewes, they banter with the shepherdess. They ask when she is going to get some proper size sheep, not 'these overweight grannies'.

The ewes are clipped on their backs wedged between the legs of the shearer to begin with. As the clipping progresses the ewe is turned but the shearer must be careful not to let the ewe stand or get a grip with its feet and escape. The blades of the clippers are sharp and if the shearer doesn't follow the line of the skin the clippers can cut the skin and leave a ewe nicked and bleeding. Each wound is a potential place where a bluebottle can lay its eggs.

As each ewe is clipped, Steve is carefully folding the fleeces. The ewe is gently allowed to stand and it walks off. Its dignity shattered and its fleece gone.

After lunch, she sends the Steve off to exercise the dogs. The first weeks he just took Kipper on a lead as the shepherdess suggests this might be easier. But this week, he is taking both dogs and going further.

It is a beautiful May afternoon. The hedges, the heather and the hills, the fells and the ferns are just bursting into life after a winter of dormancy. Everywhere the fresh, new shoots of almost edible greenness are colouring the landscape. The air is fresh and little wind. It is a perfect day to enjoy the hills, to really experience what freedom could be after twelve years.

He walks out from the farm, a dog on a lead in each hand, Kipper pulling, desperate to get up on the hills, and Queenie full of tongue-licking obedience walking at his side. The years of Queenie's training before she retired to Joyce has made her a joy to walk – unlike Kipper. Off up the road, they go, all eager in their own way to explore the hills. It is Queenie whose enthusiasm for the hills will be his undoing and change his life.

They head for Rowling End, past the run-down shell of the purple house at Rigg Beck and up towards the path to Causey Pike. The shepherdess has told him that the path that circles Causey is a great walk. As they walk, the birds flit ahead of them and the ewes keep a wary eye, the lambs hiding behind their mothers as the trio cut off the road and head upwards.

Once off the road, and when he feels sure that there are hardly any sheep within any distance, he lets first Kipper and then Queenie off the lead. Queenie stays by his side like an obedient foot soldier trained to follow his ankle. Kipper explores. Explores with his nose, with his ears, with his eyes and twists this way and that as he finds one scent followed by another. A dog in continuous motion on the hillside – twisting and turning with every smell and scent, as he soaks up the pleasure of the open fell.

The prisoner is unwinding. He has been in over a dozen prisons in his dozen years inside. He never imagined, never dared to dream that he could find himself on a hillside as the world burst into life after a winter of cold and dark. His mind is like his body. Just as his body has been cooped up and restrained, his mind has not dared to reach beyond the confines of what might seem possible. He cannot believe he is out walking, on a hillside, with two dogs at his side.

As he makes his way up the hillside, he begins to let his mind wander. He relaxes. As he climbs more he can feel the race of his heart and the warmth of his own body heat on a late spring day. He begins to sweat with the exercise. He has worried about this walk, worried about how this walk might be – the responsibility of the dogs and the sheer agoraphobic freedom of the open sky. Meanwhile, little by little the dogs sense his relaxation and begin to wander further from his side. Even Queenie begins to pause as she picks up the scent of sheep and the fragrance of the chase.

As the path climbs he cuts across to the left, so he can reach the saddle of the pass. At the saddle, he stops and is dizzy. Behind him, he can see the majesty of Catbells and the grace of Maiden Moor, next to it High Spy and the mess of Dale Head. Below is the neat shape of the Coledale Valley with the winding stream running down the middle. He stops to rest on a rock and catch his breath before deciding whether to go up and conquer the knuckles of Causey Pike, or take the sensible route for a man who has not walked this far and this high in twelve years which is to avoid the summit and follow along the downhill route of High Moss and the cranny that runs between Outerside and Causey.

The decision is taken from him. The dogs – where are the dogs? He looks around him frantically. Queenie is behind him, mooching in the bracken, but he cannot see Kipper anywhere. In a few seconds, he goes from mind-wandering serenity to blind panic. He knows what the dogs mean to Joyce.

He looks around him, his eyes searching everywhere in panic. In the distance, he sees a woman peering in the bracken with what looks like a dog at her feet. She is down in the direction that he was going to go. He runs. He hurtles down the narrow path towards the woman and the dog. He leaps through the vegetation cutting through the burgeoning bracken. As he runs, his foot hits a rock and he sprawls headlong. His arm hurts but he picks himself up and runs again. Soon he is close enough to see the woman and what look like two dogs. Her back is to him.

He shouts, 'Kipper, Kipper, KIPPER!'

Kipper's head pops up, and he looks at him with the look of faint puzzlement in which dogs specialise. 'Is something the matter? Come and see what I have found. It's dead good,' says the look on Kipper's face.

'Ah. Is he yours?' the woman says on seeing him approach. 'I wondered where he had come from. The two of them found a rabbit and chased it down this hole. I've been struggling to get them away from it. Could you help? Perhaps you could put him on a lead. My Rose loves nothing more than to chase a rabbit.'

He grabs Kipper by the collar and puts his lead on. Kipper's face changes from the excitement of the chase to the annoyance of the capture.

'What is your dog called? Kipper? Mine is called Rose.'

'Yes, Kipper. They've both got a bit muddy with the digging, haven't they?'

'What's a walk without getting dirty? Eh? Rose loves her walks. How often do you bring Kipper out here?'

The prisoner's mind goes blank. A moment ago, he was in sheer panic about losing Kipper, now it has changed to another emotion. Rose's owner is gorgeous, at least, as seen through the eyes of a prisoner for whom female contact in the last twelve years has been very, very limited. She is young, maybe late twenties or early thirties, and tall, nearly his height and slender with long slim limbs. Hazel eyes, brown hair in a page-boy cut, big round alert eyes and a lop-sided smile which appears out of her beautiful, almost impassive face.

'I am sorry. What did you say?'

'How often do you bring Kipper out here?'

'Well, not enough,' he says, and pauses. What can he say next? That he is in prison the rest of the week? 'I only really walk the dogs on a Saturday afternoon.'

'Dogs?' she asks.

'Oh shit,' he cries, and his eyes open wide with the acknowledgement. 'Yes, there are two of them. Kipper and Queenie. Where is Queenie?'

'Queenie?'

'She's more like a sheepdog – well, she is an ex-sheepdog,' he says, and starts jogging back towards where he last saw Queenie, when he was sitting on the rock, day dreaming. 'Sorry, I need to find her,' he calls back over his shoulder.

He gets back to the rock, but Queenie is nowhere to be seen. A few moments later, Rose's owner catches up with him.

'No sign of her? What does she look like?'

'She's a collie.' His eyes frantically search the hillsides either side of the saddle. All he can see is a few sheep lumbering across the hillside...

'Is that her?' asks Rose's owner. 'Back down towards Rowling End. It looks like there's a sheepdog rounding up those sheep.'

Watching the panic in this man's face, she has to work hard to suppress a smile. She has been snatching glances at his face as he has scoured the hillside. He has a handsome face, a little like that tennis player, whose name she can never remember. She feels in his eyes there is both sadness and kindness – and right now alarm. He seems skinny and somehow out of place. She's amused by seeing this grown man in such a panic. And he is, well...her train of thought is interrupted.

'Oh no, oh no, oh no. Oh, you are right. She's rounding up the sheep.' He sets off down the side of the saddle to fetch Queenie. 'I am sorry. I'd better go.'

'Would you like my help?'

He hesitates, unable to decide what is right or proper or anything. 'Er, sure.' He heads quickly towards the scree-sided slope, only stopping to drop Kipper's lead and say, 'Please bring Kipper with you.'

'Queenie, come here. Queenie, come here,' he shouts at the wayward dog. She ignores him even as he gets closer, if anything quickening her pace. 'Queenie, come here.' He lunges after the sheepdog, taking giant bunny hops across the hillside and over the stream, but missing with one foot that crashes full into the water. He heaves himself up the other side and keeps running after the sheepdog.

Rose's owner watches in a mixture of amusement and amazement. He is catching up on Queenie but still she eludes him.

'Try saying, "That'll do",' she yells across the fifty yards that separate them. He looks up, perplexed.

'What?' he shouts over his shoulder.

'Try saying, "That'll do" to her.'

'Queenie, that'll do,' he shouts in desperation.

And, like the adult owner of a new computer who is told what to do by their seven-year-old, he is both embarrassed, mortified and delighted when Queenie stops instantly chasing the sheep and stays where she is. Those three simple words have unlocked the code to her obedience, magically, immediately, amazingly.

The sheep Queenie has been chasing slow down to a walk and look on bemused. He catches up with the recalcitrant dog and puts her collar on. He would scold her. He would whack as hard as he could to vent his anger. But he is afraid he will make some other basic sheepdog error in front of this woman. So he simply spits out as he bends over, 'You fucking dog, you fucking dog,' very quietly, while trying to force a smile.

She catches up with him and hands him back the lead for Kipper.

'Thank you. Thank you very much.'

'No problem, no problem at all. She is just doing what she's been trained all her life to do and perhaps you can forget about that job application to be a shepherd.'

He laughs but behind the outward good humour his mind is in turmoil. This is conversation, normal conversation with a woman. She's not the shrink or the prison officer from Dartmoor or the ageing dinner ladies from a thousand prison kitchens. She is a woman, a woman of his age, a woman he thinks is pretty, and a woman who has been helpful and kind. A woman he could hold. But he isn't with his workmates and now he just has to make conversation. The lies just start to tumble out.

'No, my mum tends to do the dog walking. I shouldn't have brought her but she doesn't get much exercise so I took pity on her. I won't bring her next week.'

'I'm surprised I haven't seen you before. I am out on the hills most Saturdays. I work Saturday mornings and then Rose and I come and walk the hills. We are creatures of habit. I am not up for this fell-counting business. That bloody Wainwright has a lot to answer for with all his guide books. I have about half a dozen fells I like – Grizedale is one of my favourites and the loop up from Rowling End. I am so sad the Purple House is going.'

She pauses to catch her breath.

'I like High Spy and Maiden Moor. It's so beautifully flat up there and the views over Derwentwater and towards Skiddaw are stunning but I always avoid Catbells – too many people. The first swifts are back and are meant to be back on High Spy so we might go there next week. Isn't that right, Rose?'

He is just beginning to lose interest; he doesn't care where she walks next week. But then he realises. She is telling him. She is telling him where she will be…where she will be next week, so they can meet again. The fireworks have become images of rusty seized-up joints. He has been banged up for too long.

'Right then. Well, thank you. I don't know what I would have done today without your help. I'll see you around.'

And, with that, he marches off down the hill with the two reluctant dogs in tow.

Saturday 15th May

On the following Saturday, when Joyce says to walk the dogs, he is no longer unsure or reluctant. Instead, he is as keen and pulling as hard on the end of his mental leash as Kipper is pulling on his real one.

Of course, he has to do battle with Joyce on why he shouldn't take Queenie. He is about to lie when he realises that the truth is far more powerful – she chased the sheep.

So, he and Kipper are off for their walk. In the week since his last meeting with Rose and her owner, he has done his best to fill up on conversation. A week ago, he had no idea who Wainwright was, now he can tell you everything he had to say about this mountain. He knows the best route up the back of High Spy. He knows about the swifts and the wheatears of early spring. He knows where the name High Spy originated. He knows about the graphite in the Borrowdale valley and how in its heyday the valley was an economic powerhouse of the whole area and that the term black market comes from the graphite trade.

The weather is not quite as good as the spring balm of a week ago. The wind is blowing from the north east and the clouds are grey. As he and Kipper begin the steep ascent to High Spy the first spits of rain fall. Not hard. Not enough to stop but not the best weather for a walk.

Kipper is oblivious to the turmoil the prisoner is feeling and the rain that has just started. He is shoving his snout in the piles of dead bracken and savouring the whiffs of mouse, vole and rabbit. This dog is just happy to be on a walk.

But the walk to the top of High Spy takes longer than he thought. When he gets to the top he looks for her figure. He cannot see her. He walks towards the far end in case she is just out of sight.

Kipper is unhappy at being pulled along and the prisoner is distraught at her absence. As he crosses the flat top of Maiden Moor and heads for High Spy, he catches sight of a slight figure heading away. He quickens his pace. He is now almost running and Kipper is feeling cheated. A walk is not a walk if there is no time to sniff and double back, to chase dead-end smells, no time to investigate the thousand things that people cannot hear or smell or sense about a hillside.

As he gets closer to the figure he starts to wave and shouts a greeting. The figure turns and he realises that it not her but a woman twice her age and has to mumble an apology. He is downcast.

'So now I know that you chase lots of women when you are out walking, and I thought I was special!'

He turns around and she is there. He cannot work out where she has appeared from. Rose and Kipper wag tails and circle each other sniffing. Kipper likes Rose. The prisoner would kiss Rose's owner too if he could.

'You walked straight past me,' she adds, but she is smiling that lop-sided smile of hers.

'Don't tell me that,' he says. 'I thought you must have changed your plans.'

'If truth be told, I was on my way back down when I turned and just caught sight of you on the skyline so I came back up.'

'I did have trouble getting all my jobs done and the walk up took longer than I expected. Kipper wants to smell every plant, every rabbit hole and chase every bird.'

'Of course, that's what they do.'

Their conversation alone doesn't do justice to their meeting: to see their eyes as they savour each other's faces with glances that don't turn away; their body language as they enjoy each other and circle each other teasing, just encroaching into each other's personal space.

'I am afraid I have to be getting down. I am parked in Grange. Shall we try and do better next week? We could walk to Seatoller and back. The high route on the way there and the low route on the way back.

'That sounds good to me.'

'Shall we meet at 2 p.m. by the church? There should be parking space near there. What do you say?'

'I say it sounds good to Kipper and me.'

When she has set off down the hill and is out of sight, he lets out a loud yelp of delight. He has a date with a woman, well a sort of date. As he and Kipper walk he is smiling. This is why prisoners go on day release, to be reintroduced to the real world. And that is just what he is doing.

10: The first dance

Monday 31st May

It is half term at school. The fell-runner's routine is now established. First, he runs, and then he ends up at the farm where he helps with some jobs and feeds his lamb. Jessica is now as big as Kipper and much heavier. On this particular day, he knocks on the door of the farmhouse and goes in. Joyce is at the kitchen table reading the newspaper and listening to the radio. The radio is always on, he thinks.

In the kitchen, he mixes up two litres of milk from the powder on the sideboard while he chats to Joyce. He is making one litre for now and one litre for later on as he leaves.

'Jessica doesn't really need it, you know,' Joyce says without looking up from the newspaper.

'How do you mean?' he asks.

'She doesn't need the milk any more. She is eating the grass and she'd be fine without it.

He pauses before he replies, 'Well, she loves drinking it and I like feeding it…if that's okay.'

'Of course it is. It'll make her a better weight for market.' Now Joyce is looking up to see how he reacts. She has a twinkle in her eye which he notices.

He has not thought about what might happen to Jessica. Inside his stomach has tightened.

'Can't you breed from her?'

'Ah, that's another thing I should told before. She is a he! Jessica is male. Do you biology students know the difference between boys and girls?'

'What! Now you are just messing with my head. I will kidnap Jessica and take her to live in my bedroom before I let you send her to market.'

He can't decide whether she is serious or not, on either count. He takes the milk and heads for the sheep shed.

Jessica knows his voice and when he calls Jessica she comes running to the gate. As Joyce said, the lamb is starting to eat grass out in the fields, and loves her bottles. Her head bobbing, she forgets to breathe as she drinks and the milk stops as a vacuum forms. Then puzzled she lets go and the air rushes in and she guzzles again. This pattern repeats itself till the litre of milk is all gone.

As she feeds, he talks to her. He talks to her about nothing, about how he wants her to meet the other Jessica at school, and how she is like Jessica, his mother, because they both like their food and are a little the heavier for it!

When he has finished feeding her, he walks round the fields with the ewes. Six months ago, he had barely seen a sheep, but is now a country boy at home with the ewes. They too are at home with him. They are wary of him, but wary not frightened. He can walk within twenty feet without them running. All the time Jessica follows him, obediently, demurely, hopefully, that another feed may come soon.

At the top of the field he pauses. He loves the view from here. It is the place where the ewe gave birth in the depths of

January, when our story began. But he doesn't know that. He just knows that the Newlands Valley spreads out before him. He watches the sky full of late April showers in May. He watches as the clouds drive across the skyline. He watches as the patches of bright sunshine are chased across the hillside and the felltops by the patches of shadow.

When he has taken his moment, given his mind the time to tumble dry on all the thoughts in his head, he goes back to the farmhouse and the shepherdess and makes them both a cup of tea.

In a strange quirk of the way that two people can get to know each other, listening to music has become a part of their weekly ritual. The shy, gawky, teenager and the grey-haired lonely lady push and pull at each other's boundaries through music. Each week they tease and tantalise each other with their choices. Above all they want the other to hear their music and enjoy it. Yet neither will say it like that. Neither will openly admit that they like what they have heard. The game is to let the other into their world, but never get caught admitting they enjoy it.

In the living room, they sit in the two old armchairs whose wooden arms and frayed covers are a good indication of their use and age. This week he goes first. He chooses Adele's 'Someone Like You', a song whose words inspire and terrify him. He can hear her pain. He can imagine his pain if Jess loved someone else and all he could do was to try and find somebody who was like her. Sometimes he worries that he doesn't like the same music as his peers. For him, there is no hip hop or rap. It is hard to imagine that Joyce would have had any interest or tolerance of listening to that kind of music. For Joyce, too, can hear the emotion in Adele's voice and she too brings the song back, circling into her own life.

But it is her choice that is electrifying. At his prompting, she has upgraded to a CD player, with even a jack where he can plug in his iPod. She has been to Workington and bought her favourite CDs. Amongst them is Puccini's *La Bohéme*.

Many of Joyce's choices are centred around love. This is no coincidence. It is love that drove her to these hills. It is love that she misses. It is love for which she yearns. Now she introduces him to the intensity of the two loves in *La Bohéme*. As always, she tells him the story of the music as it begins.

'This is the story of two people in love. But theirs is a love that cannot be. He is a poor poet. Neither of them has any money. She has a terrible disease. So he tries to push her away. This is the scene where his flatmate is flirting with another woman. It's a waltz.'

As the music plays, as he listens, as she shuts her eyes, the dance fills him. He can imagine himself dancing. He imagines himself dancing with Jess showing their passion. Even their love fills his imagination. As the music finishes, he sighs.

'I wish I could dance. I wish I could dance to music like that.'

'Actually it's a song more than a dance. But I did learn to dance to music like that.' She pauses. 'When I was nineteen, maybe twenty, young women from rich families, or whose families were ambitious for them like mine, learnt how to be ladies. We weren't expected to have careers. We were expected to be ready to be wives, we prepared for that life. We learnt to dance, we learnt how to prepare meals and lay the dinner table.'

'So you were once able to be tidy! I don't believe it. And you can dance – like properly?'

'I'll ignore that comment, you cheeky young man – and I did still train to be a nurse', she retorts. She then adds, 'The tango. I can certainly dance the tango still. That was always my favourite. The tango can either be a lion or a lamb. It can be the dance of lovers or of grandmothers. So, while old ladies see it as a gentle tea dance, I saw it as a way to get close to men at a time when that kind of contact was frowned on. I could move up close…'

'Joyce. Stop! Really! Could you teach me to dance the tango? Like we were grannies?' he adds emphatically.

'Of course I can. Now? Actually, yes now. I haven't danced the tango for years. Let's push the chairs back. Let's see what I can remember. I will teach you.'

He watches her, amazed. He can see she is energised. He can see the bursting form of a woman thirty or forty years younger in her eyes.

'The secret of the tango is all about swings of emotion. If you watch people doing the tango one minute they are close, then distant, then flesh pressed close, and then spurned. So, first of all, you must learn to stand. Stand and look into my eyes. Put your left hand into the small of my back and with the right hand hold me up here. Now let's just stand a moment. Be comfortable with our closeness. And now push me away with your left hand but keep holding on your right hand. So, push me away and now pull me back. And look into my eyes. We are play fighting turned into dance. That's good.'

'Now push me away, and pull me back, but make me go on past you – move to one side like a bull fighter. I am charging you and you must sidestep me. That's it. Now let's practise again. Imagine I am the woman of your desires. You've come to kiss and I lean back so I can evade your kisses. My leg goes up, well it used to!'

Two people dancing. Two very different people are dancing. He is tall and skinny. She is shorter and striking, if faded features, as she dances, a younger woman emerges. The beautiful woman that she was forty or more years ago: the beautiful eighteen-year-old debutante, the belle of the ball, the woman all the men chased. At eighteen she and he today would have been the perfectly matched couple. Now, after the end of her marriage, after the fall-outs with her children, after the loneliness of being a farmer, she is no longer eighteen.

After half an hour of practice, of back and forth, they stop. Her legs are sore. His brain is full.

At home, his mother and sister are watching bank holiday specials on the telly when he returns. Usually, he does not join them, instead preferring to listen to music or do games on the playstation. Today is different because they are watching a rerun of a dancing programme and, at the moment he pops his head round the door, the TV host says that a cricketer is to perform a tango. He stops mid-sentence, does a verbal handbrake turn and says he will join them.

The fell-runner's mother and sister are amazed! They never all watch the same TV programme. Equally amazing is that he is focused on the programme. They are used to him half-watching a programme while reading a magazine or texting his friends, sprawled out on the sofa. But he is focused on the dancing. His mother does not know what to think. She wants to lift his skull and peer inside so she can work out what on earth is going on.

The last walkers are heading down off the fells on a warm, summer evening. The sun is setting on Catbells, and the orange light is colouring the fresh bracken and the heather. Inside a farmhouse in the Newlands Valley a woman, a tearful woman, dances the tango alone. She is remembering what life used to be like. She is painting her teenage years with the whitewash of perfection. As she practices her tango on her own, she is remembering how she used to make heads turn, how things used to be. And as she circles round the kitchen, the tears are trickling down her face. Dancing has picked the scab off the emotions she works so hard to bury. She is remembering the pain of why she really learnt to dance, and why she stopped.

11: Dog on a bicycle

Saturday 5th June

When Hazel suggested that they meet in Grange at the bridge and walk to Seatoller, the prisoner of course agrees. He's on day release every Saturday and Joyce always wants him to walk the dogs. Hazel has no idea how difficult what she has just suggested is for him. He has no idea how he will make it there. Hazel tells him that he can park towards the Grange Hotel. He thanks her.

Now the day has come and he has a plan. He will take the bicycle he uses to get from the prison to the farm and cycle to Grange. He will persuade Kipper to run alongside him and he will be able to reach Grange in time.

He and Kipper set off. He can't let Joyce see him go off on a bicycle so he has left it near the farm gate. He walks off down the farm lane to the road with Kipper and at the gate, he hops onto his bicycle and puts Kipper on the lead. This is dangerous territory for a man whose cycling skills are as recently acquired as his dog-walking skills.

To begin with he just sets off at a gentle pace. Kipper is still walking and the progress is slow but definite. Encouraged he tries to pick up the pace. Time is running out. He approaches the car park mayhem below Catbells. If it had just been him and Kipper and no cars he would have been okay, but when the first car approaches, he can't decide what to do. He then realises that, as Kipper is behind him, even though he may pass the car in the narrow gap, Kipper won't necessarily. So, he stops again and pulls Kipper in on a shorter lead. He decides to walk Kipper round till the worst of the cars are out of the way. He and Kipper can then put on a decent pace once they are on the Catbell Terraces, or so he thinks.

On foot, it takes him ten minutes to negotiate the cars. At the Terraces, he remounts the bicycle and tries again. This time he talks to Kipper encouragingly: 'Come on, boy, come on, boy, let's go.'

They begin well with Kipper running alongside him as he cycles. They progress several hundred yards like this, at a decent pace, and his spirits are up, but then Kipper smells something he just cannot resist and stops to investigate. In a cartoon moment, the slack in the lead takes about a second to run taut and then 'pow'. Simultaneously dog and man are airborne. Kipper is pulled off his feet by the force of the lead going taut and the prisoner is pulled backwards and off his bike.

Luckily in the cartoon moment neither man nor dog is badly hurt. Kipper is whipped forward and he yelps. The prisoner has grazed his hand where he has reached out to soften his fall. Both have injured pride. By now the prisoner is desperate and he knows he is running late.

In his desperation, he scoops up the bewildered Kipper under one arm and mounts his bicycle. Like an ancient knight on his charger he uses the slight hill to get the bicycle moving and he is off. He has never been to Grange before and, as he is no more than halfway along the Catbell Terraces, he doesn't know quite how far he has to ride. But he reckons that the slope of the terraces and the wind in his hair means he is now making progress.

It is quite easy to ride downhill with a dog held under one arm. The peddling is minimal and so the fact that only one arm is on the handle bars is barely important. But when the downhill turns to uphill, or the distance grows too long, arms tire, co-ordination falters, concentration waivers, energy flags and disaster threatens.

And it is so for this romantic hero. His arm is tiring and, while he has passed the end of the terraces, he still has a way to go. Kipper, while initially quite pleased with his new method of travel, begins to tire too and to fidget. By the end of the Lake, at the back of Grange, on a gentle uphill slope, the man riding on a bicycle with a dog under one arm comes to a shuddering halt. He decides not to try riding again, and runs with Kipper on the lead and the bicycle handlebars in the other hand.

More than ten minutes late, out of breath, sweating he arrives in Grange. He slows to a walk and, like a late candidate for a job interview, he straightens his hair and checks his appearance in a car window. Then, with the right degree of hurriedness, he walks up towards the church.

To his horror, he realises that he may be too late. At the tea shop and the church there is no sign of her. He walks to the bridge and there is still no sign of her. He then walks back again to the church and to his infinite relief, he spots Rose tied to a post outside the public toilets. He waits outside as if nothing had happened.

Moments later, she reappears.

'There you are. I was beginning to think you had stood me up.'

He has not even had time to think of an excuse.

'Sorry. Sorry. I am so sorry I am late. I had trouble…parking.'

'Oh, you must have driven straight past a couple of spaces. There was one next to me when I got here twenty minutes ago.' She is just pretending to be annoyed, though; she is really just glad that he has not stood her up.

'Me and Rose didn't want to walk alone. Rose has been looking forward to seeing Kipper. I realised when I was waiting that it would make sense for us to swap mobile numbers then we can text each other if we are running late.'

A look of horror must have shot across his face. Prisoners have to keep mobiles hidden from the authorities. But that is not an excuse that he can give her.

'Is that a problem?'

'No, no, not at all. I can just never remember my number and I didn't bring it with me today. That was daft. If you give me your number, I will text you. Promise.'

'Okay, I'll write it on your arm. I haven't got a piece of paper.'

'Oh, it's probably better on a piece of paper.'

He finds a rota for the kitchens and turns a blank side out. He doesn't want a number on an arm that one of the prison officers or his fellow inmates could spot and then ring.

'Oh, okay. So it's 07956...' She says as she writes the number.

He holds the paper firmly while she writes, so that she can't open up the sheet and see that next Wednesday and the Wednesday after that he is meant to be working all day in the prison kitchens.

'There you go, but there is one thing. What is Kipper's owner called?'

He looks at her blankly, wondering for a moment why she wants to know the shepherdess's name.

She tries again, looking at him with embarrassment and bewilderment. 'What is your name?'

'Oh, sorry. It's Steve.' He also realises that he doesn't know her name.

'And yours?'

'Hazel...I am sure I've told you that before.'

All week, Steve has been practising his conversation. Prison conversation is often limited and in his talk with Hazel some of those topics are, well, off limits, like which prisons he has been to, when might he get parole, has he got any porn, does he want to trade cigarettes for chocolate?

'You have the advantage on me, you know. All I know is just how good you are with a collie that wants to be a sheepdog. I have no idea what you do. Indeed, I know very little about you.'

This is scary territory. He had not expected to be asked such a direct question. He bats it back to gain time.

'Well, all I know is you're a dog owner! Where do you live? You aren't from these parts.'

'You are a mysterious one,' she retorts. 'Let's walk. And I'll tell you about me if you promise you'll tell me all about you. Is that a deal?'

He nods.

'Well, I am thirty-two and I have lived here for a few years now, but I was born down south. I have always been an estate agent. The money is good and I love looking into the lives of the people who have the big houses. I am a nosey person. I love seeing the people who look round houses. I can tell within about a minute of starting a tour what kind of people they are. Who wears the trousers? How do they make the decisions? Moving house is such a big decision. Every viewing is a peek into people's lives.'

'Do you have a favourite house? One you would like to live in?'

'Oooh, that's a personal question.' She pauses. 'There are two on the market at the moment that I really like. Both wonderful – one is a grand house built by the Victorians in the middle of Keswick. All full of beautiful slate and grandeur. The other is a newer house built high on the Catbells Terraces. It's modern, well 1930s, but stunning. The view from the main bedroom looks right out over the lake. Imagine waking up to that every day.'

She pauses again and turns to him. 'Enough about me. I want to know about you.'

He laughs nervously. 'What is there to tell? I am a farmer. Well, to be precise, my mother is a farmer. She farms sheep in the Newlands Valley.'

She pulls his arm to stop him. He turns, and they stand facing each other.

'You! You are a farmer. I don't believe it. You were rubbish with your sheepdog the other week. You looked like you'd never seen a sheepdog before that day. You had no idea.'

He looks back at her. His mind is racing. Prison has taught him to be a fluent liar, to have a poker face.

'It's true that I am no good with the sheepdog. My mum does most of the sheep work. Er, I am more like the muscle. I do the grunt work. Drive the tractor. Shift the hay and clear out the barns. I look after the lambs. I mend the gateways and do the repairs.'

'So where's your dad?' she says and lets go of his arm, walking on. He can see the suspicion in her eyes.

'He left us a long time ago,' he replies, pleased at his own fluent lying.

'Oh, okay,' she says, shooting him a sympathetic look. 'So what kind of sheep does your mum have?'

'They are Suffolks. Yes...Suffolks mostly,' he adds, emphasising his uncertainty.

'The other farmers all think she is a bit odd,' he continues with more certainty. 'We moved here about five years ago. Mum had Suffolks down south, so we brought them with her. They are good lambers, you know. She gets a good price for them. This year she had mostly twins and she gets twice the price for a lamb that she'd get for a Herdwick or Swaledale.'

'Ooh, you are sounding nerdy now. I guess you know a girl loves to be entertained with lamb prices. How many ewes does she have?'

They talk and they walk. They build the chemistry of conversation. They discuss the weather, the birds, and the mountains. He guides the conversation into areas he has rehearsed.

It is only at the end of their walk as they have relaxed into each other's company that she asks a question that makes his stomach tie in an almighty knot. She still doesn't believe him. She has seen his frantic flailing efforts on the slopes of Grizedale and does not believe that somebody so incompetent with a sheepdog could have grown up on a farm. Her antennae are twitched so she decides to test him a little further and drops her bombshell on him.

'Can I come and see you on the farm?' She watches his eyes for their reaction.

'How do you mean?'

'You live on a farm, right. Next week I'd like to come and see you on the farm and perhaps we could walk from the farm?'

'Er, of course, that would be great.'

'You don't sound very convinced.'

'I'm sorry. I've led a sheltered life. I've never had a woman friend round before. Well, you see, I need to clear it with my mum. I don't know what she'd think. She'd be really curious and you might find her very nosey.'

'You're thirty-two going on sixteen then.'

'Somebody told me that farmers' children never grow up till they get their own farm or their parents die. I am afraid in my case it's true. Mum rules the show.'

'So, can I come and visit then? Promise not to embarrass you?'

Her eyelids flutter and she puts on her best coquettish smile; almost without realising it, she is flirting with him. He is embarrassed and feels awkward. He realises later that her flirting reminded him of Kylie when she worked in the sandwich shop. But he buries this memory almost as soon as it surfaces.

'Yes, of course you can. Can I text you to say what time and whether next week or the week after is better?'

'Sure. Rose and I will be waiting. Thank you. We've had another great walk.'

With that, she returns to her car while he waits till he is sure she has gone, before he goes to find his bike.

12: Visiting home

Saturday 12th June

The following week on Saturday, the prisoner has to get the shepherdess to take part in his plan. She must be his ally.

Once the pens are cleared, the hay put out, the lambs fed and the other chores that he has come to help with are done they sit down to lunch. This is part of their routine. In her patronising shepherdess way, she makes conversation as she might with a foreign language student. Slowly. Deliberately. Loudly.

He plays this game for a bit, then he can wait no more.

'Joyce, I need to ask you a favour. Quite a big favour really.'

'What is it?'

'I have met someone, out walking, on the hillside,' he starts slowly, deliberately.

'You mean a woman?'

'No, I mean an alien from Mars,' he says sarcastically. 'Yes, a woman.'

'All right, all right! And you like her?'

'I do, and she wants to visit where I live. I have told her that I am a farmer's son and that you are the farmer. And now she wants to visit me – at home.'

Joyce just stares at him. He doesn't know what to think for a moment. He shouldn't have asked. He starts to panic – this is all a big mistake. But then, the corner of her mouth turns up and a smile creeps across her face and, like a sun rising, the smile is followed by a chuckle. In between her laughter, she squeezes an explanation.

'I am your mother! You are my son!'

In his relief, he begins to laugh too, as he sees the funny side of what he has said and asked. A feeling, a sensation that for most people is common but in their lives, where the loneliness walks behind them both like a shadow, it is a feeling of release and wonder.

When their composure returns, she asks, 'How can I help?'

'She wants to visit me here next Saturday. She has suggested we go for a walk from here. I am not sure you should be around.'

Joyce's eyes open wide with delight. 'So, you want me to help you in your deceit. I will do anything I can. I have passed the time when I will find romance but, if I can, I will help you.'

Perhaps she should be judging him. Perhaps she should be wary of helping him to get to know a young woman, given what he is in prison for. It's hard to believe, but these thoughts never even cross her mind. He is now part of her flock, she wants him to flourish, to be happy. Any other thoughts that cut across that are deeply buried.

That evening, back at the prison, he texts Hazel to say that she can visit Newtown Turn Farm the following Saturday at 2 p.m.

Yes please, she texts back, almost straightaway. 'Rose and I will look forward to it all week. She can't wait to see Kipper again.'

When Saturday comes, he arrives at the farm earlier than the normal 9 a.m. Like a house-proud parent, he wants to tidy up the farm so it looks its best. Joyce and he have agreed that she will leave at 1.30 p.m. and will not come back before 4 p.m. They have agreed that she won't talk to 'his lady friend', as she now calls Hazel, and, if Joyce comes back and Hazel is still there, Joyce will go and find something to do in the field or the sheep shed.

For the half hour after Joyce has driven away in her clapped-out old Ford Focus, he paces and frets. He finds useless jobs to do. Hazel arrives at 2 p.m. as agreed.

When she arrives they are unsure how to greet each other. Should they shake hands? Kiss? Instead they do neither, and like two teenagers, they stand awkwardly.

She breaks the silence by saying, 'I bought some flowers for your mother.'

'Thank you. Do you want to walk first or have a look round?'

'Let's walk.' The flowers are left in the car while they embark on an uneventful, almost mundane, walk. When they return, she asks for a cup of tea. He curses. He hadn't thought that through. Joyce has made all the cups of tea up until now, so he really isn't sure where things are.

In the kitchen, he puts on the kettle. Cups? Tea?

'Where is your loo?' she asks.

'In the porch, through this room, then on the left,' he says, pointing the way.

As she leaves, he searches frantically through every cupboard. He finds the tea bags quickly. Cups. Cups. Cups. All he can find is some very fine looking cups with saucers. Why didn't he concentrate when Joyce made him a cup of tea? By the time she returns, there are two cups of tea on the table. He is feeling very pleased.

'Oh, I am being treated – Sunday best cups.'

'Only the best will do for our special visitors. My mum was very keen you had a good impression. She's like that.'

He is just beginning to relax. This is going rather well and then 'Oh,' she says, after taking a sip, 'Sugar. Could I have one sugar?'

His mind races. He had forgotten all about sugar. He kicks himself for not thinking ahead. There are two cupboards where he thinks the sugar might be.

'Of course,' he says as he walks to try out the first cupboard. 'Mum calls sugar "white death" so it's never where it should be,' he explains with his back to her.

He finds the sugar, pulls out several pieces of hay and dollops a single spoon into her cup. He is relieved that he managed to find the sugar with only a minimal fuss but aware that she noticed his unease when she asked for sugar and is puzzled.

They drink their tea as he tries to make small talk. He winces as he drinks, not daring to have sugar as he normally does in case it only increases her bemusement. She clasps her cup tightly with both hands as if her hands need warming. Her face is deadpan. She's not smiling. She tries to hoover up as much information about the farm as she can. Something is not quite right but she can't put her finger on it.

'Before we see the farm,' she asks with a mischievous grin, 'can I see upstairs? Can I see your bedroom?'

'No chance,' he retorts, 'especially on a first visit.'

'Got something to hide,' she teases.

'It's a complete mess, and there is nothing up there worth seeing,' he insists, which is much closer to the truth than she may realise. 'I am a bloke, remember. Come and see the lambs instead of my bedroom. They are much cuter, though almost as dirty.'

In the sheep shed, Jessica comes running to him. The fell-runner would be upset to see this, but for the prisoner, it is an act of salvation.

Hazel is captivated by the lamb, even though it is the size of a small Labrador now. She may live in the Lakes, but like most people, she has never met a lamb, let alone one who, like 'Mary's little lamb', follows you everywhere you go.

'Is she a boy or a girl? Can I pick her up?'

'She's a girl. Don't be daft. She weighs a ton. Perhaps you would like to feed her?'

'Really? She looks like a boy underneath.'

Joyce has left a bottle of milk made up so that her protégé can impress his girl. It *is* there on the side, standing solitary in the midst of the usual disorder. To anybody who knew the chaos and last-minute nature of the farm, it would stick out like a sore thumb, but Hazel doesn't notice.

The prisoner makes her comfortable on a hay bale. He kneels next to her and already Jessica has seen the bottle and is seeking, pumping, nudging, searching for it. At first Hazel holds the bottle too horizontal and all Jessica gets is froth and air.

He takes her hands in his and they both shiver with secret excitement at this touch. He points the teat downwards and soon Jessica has found the milk. Now she is guzzling. His touch of her hands lingers a moment longer than it needs to.

'Just let her feed. Keep that angle. Now pull the teat away so some air can get in. Watch those bubbles! Lambs are so used to having to chase every mouthful off their mothers that when they get bottle-fed they don't know when to stop so we have to feed them regularly. We can't just leave them to it.'

She is impressed. If he isn't a farmer, he knows about feeding lambs. Like most people, she will believe what she wants to believe. She will filter the world through the lens of her desires and emotions. She wants this man to be amazing. She wants him to lean over and kiss her. She wants to pull his head towards hers and let their tongues entwine, but she doesn't.

'Shall we see the rest of the farm when you have finished?'

Once the bottle is finished, he puts it on the sideboard and they tour the rest of the farm. He shows her the forcing pen and explains how they use it to separate mothers from their lambs.

They walk up to the top of the field and stand for a moment admiring the view. Before them the Newlands Valley spreads out below them. They can see Skiddaw, Little Man and Latrigg, and Carlside and Catbells. Between them they name the tops. He has rehearsed this bit of script.

They walk back down through the fields. The ewes with their lambs spread before them. Kipper follows them through the fields but the ewes mostly ignore him. He is focused on eating their droppings and Queenie has been left penned up while Hazel is visiting. Rose keeps close to her mistress's heels as wary of the ewes as they are of her.

'I'd better be going,' she says as they climb over the gate out of the last field.

'Do you want a last cup of tea before you go?' he asks. He knows he shouldn't ask her in again. Like Cinderella, as his deadline approaches he forgets himself, and Joyce returns at 4 p.m., as agreed. While the prisoner hoped for an extra half hour with Hazel, the shepherdess is keen to catch sight of this woman. Joyce doesn't just want to play matchmaker from behind the scenes. She wants to be involved.

So when they emerge, Joyce has returned and gone up to the furthest corner of the furthest field.

They can just see her and she waves at them. They wave back.

'Do you want to meet again next week?' she asks from the driving seat of her car.

'Yes please. This time, it's your turn. You can show me around one of those houses you so like. You've seen around my house, now I want to see around one of yours.'

She blushes. 'I'll text you,' she says. 'I need to make sure that nobody else is being shown around.'

And with that, she slips the car into first gear and heads off down the road to New Town.

13: Check up

Wednesday 16th June

It is Wednesday morning and Hazel is in the Cumberland Infirmary. She sits in the consulting room, waiting for the neurologist. She has been here so many times before, the staff members know her and she knows them. She resents their knowledge and their intrusion into the most intimate parts of her life.

While she waits, she reflects on the injustice of her life. She has finally met a man, a gorgeous man. He seems to like the things she likes. He likes the hills. He has a dog. He makes her smile. He makes her feel wanted. She knows there is something about him that is not quite right. Something that she doesn't understand, something mysterious, something he isn't telling her. But, in a strange way, it only increases the appeal.

Here, in the hospital, being prodded is the name of the game. Every six months, she comes here and they turn her inside out. They test her reactions and ask about her symptoms. They discuss her medications. The news is rarely good. Her illness is a life sentence. She knows that she will never be entirely free and able to live again. Sometimes she thinks about prisoners and how simple their life must be. They have an end to their sentence; they count the days, weeks and months. Hers is a counting game, but she doesn't know where she is counting to. All she knows is that she feels like real life is on hold.

Hazel has Parkinson's disease.

She has tremors and numbness. Her face is beginning to lose the smile which, as a child, everybody commented on. Sometimes she freezes, her muscles lock and she has to rock herself into action. Sometimes her walk becomes a shuffle. Her left arm loses control.

She is young to have Parkinson's. At first, she was told it was tiredness, and then hormones, and then she was told to ignore it and it would go away, but eventually the doctors took her seriously. Her GP referred her to the hospital, and so one day, three years after her first symptoms, a middle-aged man with all the warmth and compassion of a traffic warden told her she had Parkinson's. He told her that nobody knows why people get it, that there is no cure, but there are treatments and, just as the questions came flooding in, her appointment was over. And now, three years after the diagnosis, she has medication. She doesn't take her pills every day, but when muscles lock before she can even get out of bed in the morning, she takes them so she 'unfreezes' for the day ahead.

Perhaps the biggest impact on her life is how she feels about herself. Parkinson's is an old person's disease. The people who get it are old, the symptoms make people look frail and uncertain on their feet, and so now she is beginning to feel decrepit or more importantly unlovable because she will be old before her time. The worst impacts, for now, are all in her head.

So what she cannot do in real life she does in her dreams. She can dream. She can lust. She can fantasise. When she finds a man like she has on the hills, in her dreams all futures are possible. There are children. There is a beautiful house. There is the adoration of more than just her dog.

And he, the man on the hill, is the focus of her dreams. She imagines them together. She imagines them in a big house. She imagines them with young children. She imagines them together. In her dreams, they are so happy.

She also knows one day she will have to tell him. She will have to hold this man, any man, tightly and say, 'I have Parkinson's', and watch his face, read his eyes, and his reaction of bewilderment at what she is saying.

In every relationship, real or imagined, this is the big chasm she has to cross. If she had cancer, it would be easy. People understand cancer. People understand divorce and death and cancer, but Parkinson's? She will have to tell him there is no cure. There is no reason why she has it, no infection caught from unprotected sex or dirty water, just a buggered gene deep inside her cells. At least with cancer she could be declared free, but with Parkinson's, she never has that light at the end of the tunnel. She can explain the tremors and the movements, the squirming and the shakes, but she can never be free from them.

This time, the doctors tell her that the symptoms are stable. No worse, but no better. The young woman doctor is her age. She fixes her eyes on the doctor as Hazel asks her about sex, whether there are problems with Parkinson's and sex. The doctor starts a spiel about how there is no reason why people with Parkinson's shouldn't enjoy a full sex life. Some patients find regular sex reduces their symptoms. The doctor smiles painfully, and Hazel knows that she is probably painting an optimistic picture. She knows that smile from doctors which can say so much.

It is a smile which hides the fact that the years ahead will feel like the slow descent into decrepitude, when her body loses control at the crucial moment, when she needs to use two hands to clean her teeth to stop the shaking as the medicines wear off, when her pulling, tugging dog hides the risk of a shuffling gait, when her colleagues at work tell her to smile more and she wants to scream at the doctor – how can her sex life be normal when she is an old woman before her time? There are things that are better left unsaid between a doctor and their patient so she smiles back. She must continue the diet, the exercise, and the drugs: but is the emotional austerity always going to be part of her life?

Meanwhile, her fantasies will have to go on. In bed at night she dreams. The man on the fells. She dreams about making love to him. She dreams they are in the big houses. In the bright sun of a hot July day. In the deep green bracken of Carrock Fell in the pouring rain. But in her daydreams, without even realising it she is always whole. She has no symptoms, no tremors, no frozen muscles and no feelings of imperfection.

14: Down at the park

Saturday 26th June

It is a Saturday afternoon, and the prisoner and the estate agent are down in Fitz Park on a perfect summer's day. As promised, she did text him, and a fortnight later, they meet down by the fountain across the road from the ice-cream van. The shepherdess is now fully engaged in this romantic intrigue. Joyce drives him to the swimming pool and drops him off with Kipper.

'I'll pick you up here at 5 p.m.,' are her parting words.

The estate agent is waiting for him with Rose, down by the fountain, as her text said they would be. She smiles when she sees him. Rose wags her tail. This is the awkward stage of a relationship. Do they kiss when they meet? Are they 'going out' yet? She is not sure. He is not sure. He waves as they approach.

They don't kiss.

They come close. The dogs sniff bottoms. Hazel moves to kiss him but he turns his head as Kipper yelps with excitement and she kisses into thin air and he doesn't notice.

The dogs are to be bored this week. They set out to walk the loop of Fitz Park. For dogs this is the walk of suburbia, no rabbits, no bracken, and few smells. It is better than nothing but it is not the full-on walk on the fell that they are used to.

So, as the dogs mooch and do what they can to make up for the lack of excitement, their owners talk. They pause to watch the cricket. The boys and one girl in their whites are fielding. The tall oaks on the bank are in full leaf. Behind them is the mighty Skiddaw. Today just a single wispy cloud near the summit. They can see the path where a flow of invisible people toil up Jenkin Hill on the route to the top.

'One day, we must try and do Skiddaw together,' she suggests.

Once they have watched the cricket, they meander round the park. The talk comes easily. They stop at the tree with the huge lump the size of a hay bale. Steve tries to get his arms around it and fails. They join hands and still they cannot go around the tree. Again, their hands touch a moment longer than is necessary. From here, on the opposite side of the park, they can see the paragliders on distant Walla Crag and the scree slopes of Clough Head.

At the children's park, they watch together, and each silently wonders. She wonders whether this could be her one day, with children down at the park. And he wonders whether this could be the pair of them. His stomach turns at how old his daughter would be now. He knows that one day, he will need to tell her that not only is he a prisoner, but a man who killed the last woman he loved and also caused the death of his first child. But, as the children play, they talk. The dogs are still with them but now close at their heels. Bored.

Back where they started she pays for them to do a round of putting on the close-cropped grass around the tennis courts. They are both useless. Kipper tries lamely to chase a golf ball. After a while they abandon the putting and, as if on cue, she says, 'I have a surprise for you.'

He looks at her.

'You wanted to see one of my houses, one of my favourite houses. It's the old vicarage and today it's free at 4 p.m. There is a viewing at 3 p.m. but after that we could have a look at it. What do you say?' Her eyes are twinkling.

'I say let's go. After all, I have shown you somewhere I call home and I don't see why you shouldn't do the same.'

She gives him a playful nudge in the ribs.

'Cheeky. We are allowed to dream, aren't we?'

'Of course we are. Will you tell me your dreams as we go around?'

'Maybe, maybe.'

The walk from Fitz Park to the old Vicarage, Morpeth How, is short. The dogs are even more unimpressed. They are now tied up in the porch. As their owners look round the house, Kipper puts his head on his paws. His eyebrows move in time with noises from the house. Rose stays sitting, impatient with the lack of action.

'Give me the spiel,' he says. 'Pretend I am a potential house buyer. Pretend you are showing me around.'

She rolls her eyes, but actually quite likes the idea.

'Well, sir, this is the hall. It is the centrepiece of the house. This magnificent staircase acts to join upstairs and downstairs and comes with a fantastic balcony. There are very few houses of this size in Keswick and it is very rare that such a house comes on the market. Indeed, this house last came on the market over thirty years ago.

'Through here is the kitchen. I'm sure you would agree it is a spacious kitchen. You can just imagine this would be the heart of family life. This Aga is oil-fired and heats the house beautifully in winter. There is plenty of room here for a kitchen table round which a family would eat. We can imagine the daughter back from school doing her homework. We can imagine the young son playing with his cars on the floor. We can imagine the mother cooking tea, as her husband returns. As they greet, they kiss.'

By now her voice is barely louder than a whisper. They are both moved by the scene she paints. They both know she would not say this for any ordinary viewing. She is moved because she thinks it is a scene she will not see. She believes that her condition will never make it possible. He is moved because it is a scene from his past. He has been the father returning home. He has had his chance at family life. It was never so idyllic. And he cannot believe he will be allowed it again.

'Let me show you upstairs, sir,' she says to break the emotion of the moment.

She leads the way upstairs. 'There are three bedrooms along this corridor, all a perfect size for children or guests. They have their own bathroom and the views towards Barrow and Causey are wonderful. Come this way to the master bedroom.'

They cross the landing. 'This is the spacious master bedroom which comes complete with an en-suite. Note the view overlooking the lawn. While you are there, admire the sash windows which allow in plenty of light. These windows and the high ceilings make the room seem even larger than it is. Certainly, it would be easy to fit a super king-sized bed here and still have plenty of space.'

She pauses momentarily. He has been looking towards the window as she spoke. He turns to see why she has stopped but she is standing closer than he realised. His elbow pushes her and she takes a step backwards. But the bed, the large bed in the master bedroom of the dream house, is behind her. She overbalances and falls backwards onto the bed face up. This is a moment neither of them expected. She looks up at him from the bed and seizes the moment.

'Come to me,' she whispers, arms outstretched to beckon him to her. He needs no second invitation. He moves to the bed and slips into her arms. Their lips meet and they kiss. She holds his head in her hands and their tongues entwine. She then rolls over so that she is lying on top of him.

'I have wanted to do that since the moment we met,' she says.

'What, when I was showing you how not to be a shepherd?'

'You're right, maybe it was the second time we met, when you walked right past me on Maiden Moor or when you nearly stood me up at Grange. If we try again, I might remember better.'

They kiss again. This time they explore each other's bodies.

He pulls up her shirt and strokes her back. She sits astride him, her tight jeans perfectly outlining her bottom and legs. She can feel his excitement.

'I think it was the first time we met. What about you?'

'I wanted you before I even met you. Why do you think I got my specially trained dogs to be so badly behaved right in front of you?'

She slaps him playfully on the leg.

'So we have both wanted each other from early on, it's fair to say?'

'That would be fair.'

'So we have been waiting for this for a while, it's fair to say?'

'That would be fair.'

'So we shouldn't waste this opportunity? It's fair to say?'

'We shouldn't waste a moment.'

She slips her hand under his shirt. He moves to take her top off. She leans forward again so that her top can slip down over her head. But, as she does so, a distant voice calls out from downstairs.

'Hazel, are you in there?'

The voice echoes up the stairway and into the master bedroom.

They look at each other in horror. She is the first to move. She leaps up. She pulls her shirt back on and straightens her clothes as she talks.

'Oh my God. That's my boss. I am dead meat if he finds me here like this. You've got to hide. Oh no, no, no. You've got to be a client.'

'What? A client?'

'Yes, I am showing you around the house.

'I'm up here, Nigel, just showing a client round the house,' she shouts out of the room door. She turns back to her lover in waiting and says, 'Just act like you are looking around the house and I'll be back in a moment.'

With that, she disappears out of the door.

Down in the hall, she greets Nigel, trying her best not to look flustered or as if she has just been undressing in the master bedroom.

'Hello, Hazel, the Aldridges rang around 2 p.m. to say they couldn't do 3 p.m. and asked to delay to 4 p.m. and they're a little late. I didn't realise we had another client to show round.'

'Oh, I'm sorry, the client came direct to me late as well, so I said I would show him round.'

'Oh right...Who is the client and what are those dogs doing outside the front door? I recognise yours. But dogs at a client house? Hazel, what is going on?'

His tone is terse, but quiet enough so that his clients can't hear.

'It was a...Mr Smith. Oh Nigel, I am really sorry about the dogs. I am looking after one for a friend and I didn't think there was anybody else coming to visit the house today.'

He looks at her quizzically and she knows he is perplexed by her behaviour. She hopes the fact that she is normally his most reliable agent will go in her favour.

'I had better go and see how the client is getting on,' she says and disappears back upstairs.

Back in the bedroom she finds him examining the curtains in minute *detail*.

'What are you doing?'

'Looking around the house, as directed.'

'Not like that. Come on. Let's get out of here.'

She leads the way downstairs and walks over to Nigel.

'Nigel. We're done here. Perhaps I can leave you to lock up, please?'

'I'll see you Monday, Hazel, and we can talk about today.'

15: Dancing classes

Tuesday 6th July

It is the first week in July. The exam season is over. The A Level students have all gone. Gone to celebrate and forget about school for ever. Year 12, the lower sixth, are having a week or two of activities and lessons, where the pace slows and experiences of life are broadened.

Today, a dance teacher has come to the school. In the morning, she has taken Year 10, fourth year, with the help of three other class teachers, through a whirlwind introduction to the world of ballroom dancing. This afternoon, it is the turn of year 12.

Ten years ago, this kind of lesson would never have been popular. The advent of TV shows on dancing has changed the way that schoolchildren see this kind of activity. There are still the fans of singing, rather than dancing, who stand arms folded, and the children who through embarrassment and flat feet, remain impassive. The girls are keener than the boys. The girls see the romance of dance, where the boys tend to see, well, the girliness of it. The government is keen to get children dancing, as part of a 'balanced active healthy lifestyle' so they pay for the dance teacher to go around and enthuse children about dancing.

The teacher is use to changing children's minds about dance. She is a thirty-something Spanish woman called Cristina. She has the high cheekbones and the dark hair from her Spanish roots, and truth be told, the boys are more attracted by her than by the dancing. Cristina's patter begins simply.

'Who can name some famous dancers?'

'Kara Tointon.'

'Gavin Henson.'

'Fred Astaire.'

'Ginger Rogers.'

'The man from hole in the wall.'

Laughter. The children are beginning to warm up. The names come to over twenty in total.

'Does anybody know what Gavin Henson did before he was a dancer?'

She listens as some students call out an answer. 'Yes, of course. That's right. He was – he *is* a rugby player. He played for Wales. What are the dances that these people do?'

This time the list grows much more slowly.

'Foxtrot – yes, that's right. Tango – good,' says Cristina in her slight Spanish accent. 'Okay, not easy naming the dances is it? What about the rumba or the swing? Has anybody heard of the merengue? No. What about the waltz?' A few nods at this one. 'Good.'

She smiles round at them. 'Well, today I am going to let you have a go at two dances called the swing and the tango. I am going to show you some clips of children in the United States taking part in a dance competition. I am also going to show you a clip of Antonio Banderas doing the tango so you can see just how much dancing can impress people. How dancing can be cool.'

As she says these last words, the teenagers are quiet, with a few suppressed giggles and a lot of smirking. Teachers don't use words like sexy which means she has broken, deliberately, an unspoken rule of school, and now their attention is raised.

'So, watch this clip from a documentary called *Mad Hot Ballroom* about these dance competitions in the States. What they have discovered is that ballroom dancing can help children do better at school, get into trouble less and enjoy school more. This is the final of all the schools in New York. I am going to show you first the swing and then the tango.'

They watch the first clip and they see children, younger than them, dancing with energy, grace and passion. The lower sixth see the excitement of these kids.

The clip ends and Cristina starts. 'Right, now I am going to talk you through the dance steps for both the swing and the tango while we watch those clips again. Find a partner, please. Don't worry whether they are a boy or a girl.'

'The swing is a dance. It's a fun one. It's not about slow close dancing; it's about really enjoying yourself. See how the kids are smiling. They can't frown or look like they are concentrating or they will lose points, so they hold their partners and it's the top half of their bodies that do the moving. The boy twirls the girl and they put all their joy into their dancing.

'It's three simple moves; the swing, the twirl and the embrace. So now, find yourselves a partner and I will demonstrate the steps, so I will need a volunteer to help me.'

The fell-runner looks around. He cannot decide what he thinks about the swing. He had not come to school thinking he would be practising skills he learnt at Newtown Turn Farm, but now his worlds are colliding. In the Queen's Hall, he has discovered that a dance he has danced on his own many times is going to be demonstrated and then practised by his year. Jess is here, of course. He wonders what it would be like to dance the tango with her, but he is sure she never thinks about him, let alone considers him as her dance partner.

The embarrassed boys and the excited girls pair up. He is paired with a girl called Rebecca, who is also in his Geography class.

'Smile,' says Cristina, 'and twirl your partners. Now hold her hand and rock your body from side to side. Be happy. Put yourself into it. Don't be shy, don't be half-hearted.' She is talking to a room full of unenthusiastic swing dancers.

'Okay, thank you. Back to your seats. Dancing requires people to forget about their worries, to forget about looking or feeling foolish. When you leave those behind, your dancing will be much more fun. Now, I want you all to close your eyes. I want you to imagine your fear of people laughing and that embarrassment and shyness is a little devil sitting on your shoulder. That devil keeps telling you to be shy. Can you see him? Right, now take that devil and give him a great big slap and whack him into the corner of the room. Okay, now open your eyes.'

The room of teenagers look at her. Some have sniggered and chattered, or been on their phones, throughout. Others are opening their eyes as if they have been asleep.

'Thank you, Year 12. Now I'll show you the tango. First of all, I want to show you a clip from a movie. This is Antonio Banderas, the Spanish movie star, dancing the tango with his co-star in the movie *Take the Lead*.'

The fell-runner realises, to his horror and wonder, that this is the movie he stumbled across when he returned from dancing with the shepherdess. He knows which scene she will show. He is delighted and horrified, appalled and exultant.

Cristina shows the clip. This is not the tango of elderly ladies and tea dances, but the tango of lovers and bodies in their prime.

It is the dance of seduction. Year 12 are transfixed. What they have just seen Antonio Banderas and Marilyn Allen dance is so far from where their prejudices have started the day. They all want to see, to take part in, and to feel a tango like that.

'There you go,' says Cristina, 'Now I need a volunteer.'

This is his dance. Without thinking, he stands. There is a murmur of amazement. The fell-runner is still an enigma to most of his year. He is tall and skinny and his mass of messy hair stands out a mile away. It's part dreadlocks and part tangle bird's nest. But he has presence; he is a very good-looking boy. He is also a grumpy loner, as far as many of the year are concerned. So to see him standing, volunteering to do a dance, is no less amazing them than if their taciturn, shuffling headmaster had volunteered to do the same.

'Hi,' says Cristina, 'what is your name?'

'Ashley.'

'Great, Ashley, thank you for volunteering. Have you danced the tango before?'

'A little bit, but not properly.' He is suddenly aware that the entirety of Year 12 is looking at him, and doesn't know why he stood up.

'Do you feel confident enough to show the class how to tango?'

He laughs. 'Yeah, let's have a go.'

Cristina puts on the music. Cristina and Ashley stand together in the embrace for tango. There are a thousand things that could go wrong with this kind of dance. Dancing with a partner is something that most people practise a hundred times before they show the rest of the world, but today, this unlikely couple click. She leads and he follows. She talks him through the steps with brisk efficiency.

As the music progresses, the two of them move as though they are one. He moves his head towards her neck and she leans over backwards. He flings her away and then, as if at the final moment, he pulls her back. They hold each other tightly and then spin away. Their feet move as one as his feet follow hers. She wraps her leg around his and then she lets go.

If she were a teacher at the school, the head might be having words. But this is no longer a dance class. Both of them have forgotten where they are and are just moving to the music. He who has never danced with anyone but the shepherdess before, and this dance teacher who gives the same lessons a hundred times a term, are now dancing as one.

Year 12 is enraptured. It is a moment in time which many of them will remember for years to come.

The music stops and the dance ends. For a moment, there is silence, and then the room is filled with enraptured applause and cat-whistles. The fell-runner started dancing as a nobody and finished it as a somebody. Cristina looks slightly embarrassed, and the teachers from the school awkward. She too feels that this was a performance that went beyond teaching and into the intimacy of true dance. For dancers, their intimacy is part of the occupation. For seventeen-year-olds and their dance teacher, it is not.

'Wow. Ashley. Goodness me. That was great dancing. Ashley, thank you so much,' she says, and then, regaining her composure, 'Let's give a big hand for Ashley.'

Battling with the applause and wolf whistle she adds,

'Now, Year 12, it's your turn to try out the tango. We'll just do the basic steps. Find yourself a partner of the opposite sex.'

There is a mêlée. For Year 12, dancing the tango has taken on a whole new meaning. This is not a mere time-filling, class-distracting activity. They have seen one of their number elevated in a few minutes. And, of course, all the girls suddenly want to dance with Ashley – the loner, the fell-runner…the dancer.

But he only wants to dance with Jess. His eyes meet momentarily with hers. He crosses the floor to ask her to dance, but his plans are thwarted by Rebecca who intercepts him. She figures that as she danced with him as a geek, she has earned the right to dance with him as hero. He can think of no words with which to change her mind. He throws one last forlorn look across the dance floor to his romantic heroine, and then takes hold of Rebecca, and together, they dance the tango of an elderly couple.

16. Summer sunlight

Friday 9th July

In the evenings of high summer, when the sun sets at its furthest north, a beam of sunlight, passes between the two barns and hits the old pantry window of Joyce's kitchen. It starts as a shaft on the floor of the kitchen, but as the sun sets, it cuts an arc up across the kitchen walls before it disappears when the sun sets.

At 8 p.m., the shaft illuminates Joyce in her kitchen armchair, fallen asleep while the TV plays on. The shaft of light falls on her chest. Her old fleece burred and dirty, flecked with hay from storing bales. In Joyce's life, every day must be busy, filled with jobs and chores, or else the ghosts and demons of her loneliness crowd in closer. Reminding her of her plans, for a soulmate, for a love that sang, that danced, and how they came to nothing.

Today's job has been spraying the nettles and thistles that creep into the corners of fields, so they whither and go brown. Her back sprayer filled with slushing weedkiller, she trudges into the field margins and the spots in fields where the weeds take hold. Despite the heat, she wears her boiler suit, thick gloves and wellingtons to protect her from the noxious fluid. On top of this, she wears a wide-brimmed floppy hat to protect her from the sun, but still she sweats. The dogs are locked inside the house to protect them from the chemicals.

So another day passes, and at the end of it she is exhausted, as well as itchy with the salt of the dried sweat from the day's labour. Another knackering day when she is too tired to worry, to think of what have been, to dwell on 'things'. So the shaft of light catches her on her armchair.

As she sleeps, the shaft moves onto, and over her shoulder, to the work surface. Its beam catches a teapot: a fine piece of bone china, with a delicate pattern of blue, white and gold fleck. A wedding present from more than thirty years ago now, given on a beautiful May Saturday, when the excited guests celebrated the marriage of two beautiful people. The jerky cine footage from the sixties shows the morning suits, and the smart dresses, the hats and the children in pinafore and brown sandals with white socks. A day that radiated happiness and optimism. All these years later, its only remnant is a teapot; not keeping pride of place for Sunday afternoon tea, not remembered affectionately for the people who gave it and the day it represents. It is not even used for tea, but for watering the plants.

The shaft moves on, from the teapot on the chaos of the work surface next to it. There lies a pile of ready meal cartons: chicken tikka masala, spaghetti bolognese and beef lasagne. Living alone makes cooking for one a chore. Why cook up a meal from scratch when the only company is the dogs? Ready meals are the perfect companion, quick and easy in the microwave. Take-aways are too far away in Keswick to be worth the effort. So the pile of empty cartons increases, waiting for the next trip to recycling.

Living alone does not bring either a great diet or high standards of manners and etiquette. Despite her upbringing, many, indeed most, evening meals are TV dinners. To her great delight, Joyce found a tray in a catalogue with a bottom full of polystyrene beads, which can be used to put her meal on her knees and the beads can even out so the tray is flat. The perfect solution for a TV dinner. When the meal is cooked, the dogs are allowed to lick out the empty meal cartons and which they push into a corner till each last morsel is finished.

Each evening meal is finished with a yoghurt or two. While she consumes these, the dogs prepare themselves for another licking. And when she is done, she holds out an arm each side of the armchair, a carton in each hand and lets Kipper and Queenie each lick one clean.

She has now forgotten, but it is this habit that is the root of the seemingly insignificant gap with one of her children. When her small grandchildren came to visit on one precious occasion, they too were given a yoghurt, which they too devoured. However, they were young enough to be sat on a child's chair on the floor, and Joyce had not thought to tell them or their parents that the dogs might expect to get to lick the carton. So all Queenie could see was an empty carton being waved in front of it, one she felt should be hers. So as the grandchild innocently waved the carton under her nose once too often, Queenie felt she wasn't getting her treat. Her patience snapped and she took a bite at the child's cheek. A small amount of blood was drawn. The child was terrified. The parents were horrified. Joyce was apologetic and distraught. However, when her son-in-law said the dog needed to be put to sleep, Joyce refused. She said that was an over-reaction. There was an argument and the precious family visit ended early. Joyce could not bear to put Queenie to sleep for what she saw as a minor misdemeanour. Pulled between a loss of visits from her daughter for maybe a few days a year, and the loss of a faithful companion with her every day of the year, she sided with the dog.

A few years have passed and the daughter visits again, but often without her husband, and insisting that Queenie lives in the barn while they visit. The children are big enough to eat at the table now. And the dogs still get the cartons, even if not while the grandchildren visit.

As the shaft of sunlight continues across the room and upwards, it pierces a faded picture in a tarnished silver frame. The colours have faded and the dust now covers the glass. This is a wedding photograph, not of Joyce but of her middle child, her son George. Tucked away in a corner of her kitchen, this picture is of a day she would rather forget.

This photo crystallised all Joyce's self-inflicted hurt and pain. When she left her husband Derek to find happiness, he was devastated. Her children saw his side of the story. However, as a successful cardiovascular surgeon, he soon found somebody to love him the way he liked best. It was another doctor, Sophia, fifteen years his junior; she was attractive, intelligent and devoted to him. She soon moved into her old family home, and to her it seemed as if nothing had changed. Of course, why should she care, given the choices were all hers – except when it comes to wedding days, status is critical. Who sits where? Who is in which photos?

Joyce tried to say to George that she didn't think that Sophia should come to the wedding, but lost that argument. Then she tried to say that she didn't think Sophia should be on high table or appear in the official wedding photos, but won on neither front. Her only successful battle was for a picture of just her, Derek, and George with his siblings and new bride. It was a victory of a few seconds' length, since as soon as it was taken Sophia, a heavily pregnant Sophia joined in the next picture. And she knows, from the one time she visited him after the wedding, that it is that picture that is in George's living room…

If photos were the only trauma for Joyce, then she might have happier memories of that day. She hadn't thought who she would know at the wedding, and so many people who come to weddings come as couples. She found herself outside the circle of conversation again and again, not knowing whether to barge in and feel like a bossy woman, or do nothing and feel so very alone. She knew a few of George's friends, and that they didn't want to talk to a frumpy middle-aged lady in an ill-fitting dress. She found a few family friends to chat to, but many of them were distant, conscious of her past actions. Meanwhile again and again she heard, or felt she heard, people talking about Sophia and her impending baby. There was no logic, no justification, in her feeling slighted by the choices that Derek made. But she did.

She returned home as quickly as she could. Conscious of where home now was, conscious of the unquestioning love of her dogs, conscious of the gap between her and her children. Conscious of just how great her loneliness now was.

The shaft of light is now turning orange, the rich orange of a late evening summer sunset. The light is now tracking up the wall and it scans the creams and pastel shades of the wallpaper. When Joyce moved a decade ago, she had the house decorated, and used the styles and colours of an eighties' Laura Ashley. The colours have bleached and the style dated. She never notices how the house looks as she lives with it every day, and rarely sees anything else to compare it to. Steve hardly notices the dated style – it is almost identical to how things were before he went to prison!

Over the wallpaper is a single faded child's drawing. Pinned up with blu-tack, the washed-out colours bear testament to the rare visits by her eldest grandchild. 'To Granny Joyce' they say, in careful slow letters, with pictures of a sheep, and two dogs carefully labelled 'Queenie' and 'Kipper'. The picture of Joyce showed her a little too grey and mad-looking for Joyce's liking. But a grandchild's picture is a grandchild's picture, and so up on the wall it went.

Joyce's move north came at the end of a year of pain. It started with her realisation that while she loved her husband, she wasn't 'in love' When she saw some other couples, she could see their vibrant, pulsating love. She could see that their worlds revolved around each other. With Derek, she felt none of that. She told him she was leaving to find happiness. He couldn't understand any of it, probably never did. Her children understood little more.

Joyce found this farm with her bitterly thrashed out divorce settlement. She travelled a bit, and then on a cold October day, she came north with a moving van. They moved all her furniture in, and left her alone. That evening, and many evenings after, she found herself weeping, asking herself what she had done. Casting aside the warm cocoon of suburban life for the rough and hard life of a smallholding shepherdess. How she ever thought she would find happiness, let alone a person to share her life with, nobody knows, least of all Joyce.

So here she is, asleep in her armchair, as a summer evening ends. Loneliness, not love, fills her life. The dogs keep her company, and now, to a small extent, her two new men, Steve and Ashley. Soon she will wake and shuffle to bed, once the shaft of orange light has disappeared for the day.

17: A running race

Sunday 11th July

The fell-runner is out on a Sunday morning. It is early – 8 a.m. He has established a routine where he sneaks from the house before his mother and sister are awake, goes on a long run, and then goes to help out the shepherdess. His day is Sunday, and the prisoner's Saturday, so their paths have never crossed.

It is a beautiful morning. It is cold as the sun is still climbing. He is on his favourite run; up the Coledale Valley on the old mine road, and then up over the pass and dropping down into the Newlands Valley. He is much fitter than when he first pounded this route. He can run for longer and faster. He loves his runs. He finds the pace effortless and loves the views of the fells and the climbs and descents. In running he has found a new love.

Almost inevitably as he runs his thoughts wander. They wander to the summer holidays ahead and how he will fill them. They pass by the jobs he must do at the farm. They settle on Jess and his feelings for her. Today he has not brought his iPod, but just listens to the sounds around him.

Halfway up the valley road, he is conscious of footsteps behind him. Running footsteps. He turns around and his heart misses not one but several beats. It is her. It is Jess. He stops and she does too.

'Hello! I didn't know you were a runner,' he says. It is the best opening line he can muster.

'I didn't know you were a dancer,' is her lightning reply, 'and I guess I didn't know you were a runner either.'

'Oh,' he replies lamely.

'Oh, Ash, you never cease to surprise me. There I was, thinking that you were the classic geek, and then you come out and show you can dance.'

His thoughts are in turmoil. This girl, who has filled his thoughts more or less since the moment he arrived at his new school, is now in front of him. Talking to him. Complimenting him.

'I prefer Ashley,' he says, almost to himself. His stepfather Roberto had called him Ash, and he now dislikes it as a result.

'Well, as you wouldn't dance with me the other day, you can run with me instead. I was just doing a short run to the top of Wandope. Fancy seeing if you can beat me to the top?'

'Like a race? I'm not sure I am any good.'

'Not a race, just a gentle bit of running,' she replies dishonestly. 'And I didn't think you had ever danced before our lesson the other day, so you can imagine how surprised I was. I must say, Ash, you were quite the dancer, so I'm not going to take your word that you are no good at running.'

He doesn't know quite what to say. Before he can reply, she continues.

'Oh, and if I win, you can teach me to dance. To the top of Wandope then, let's go.'

She sets off, and as in this entire encounter, he is one step behind. The first ten minutes are easy and largely flat, and he keeps up with ease. He thinks about trying to start a conversation but decides to save his breath. Just as they approach the mine, the path drops down and crosses the stream. She runs down the path and crosses it with a single bound. He mistimes his jump and his right foot splashes in the stream.

'Careless!' she says over her shoulder, as she surges up the hill.

He realises that he may be running against no mere mortal. She can run. Her pace is effortless. She has not even broken sweat. As they climb up the far side, the terrain is harder. They are both watching every step as they pick their way between the boulders and the wet patches, between the mud and the scree.

She still leads and is further ahead than she was on the mine road. By now, they have reached the crest at the head of the Coledale overhang and he is still in contention. She pushes on up the hillside, following the narrow winding path which zigzags up to the pass. He decides that he has to go for the lead. So, while Jess winds her way up the hairpins, he gets to the first bend and then heads straight up. He scrambles up the rocks and his feet are soaking but by the first bend he is ahead of her, but only just, he then pushes on to miss out another loop. This time the shortcut is steeper and longer.

'You'll regret it. There is nothing but pain in shortcuts,' she yells up to him.

He is about to reply but saves his breath.

She is right. He leaps up an enormous boulder and scrapes his shin and he is grateful for the protection that his socks and tracksuit offer. He tries again and this time makes it and he surges forward, determined not to lose the lead.

He emerges back on the main path some fifty yards ahead of her. There is about another 500 yards of steep ascent before the path levels out, and then another mile or so of climbing, to the flat top of Wandope.

His shortcut has put him back in the lead, but she is fitter and faster than he is. As they continue the steep climb, she gradually gains on him. By the time they reach the end of the climb, she is only about ten yards behind him. He is struggling while she is composed. He is covered in mud from his climb while she is clean from the knees up. He is out of his comfort zone while she is in hers.

When she is ten feet behind him she calls, 'I didn't realise I was going to have such a battle on my hands, but I will beat you, you know.'

'Not if I can help it,' he rasps back.

As the path levels out, she overtakes him. In winter this would be covered in snow, and icicles would dangle from the overhanging rocks. The path would be ice, and in summer, even hot summer, the path is wet. And, as she overtakes him, he tries to push back, but he slips and falls flat into the mud.

To his amazement, she turns and stops and comes back to him. She offers her hand to the fallen fell-runner. He accepts and she pulls him up.

'You okay?'

'Other than muddy, sweaty, and knackered, you mean?'

'What about beaten?' she asks.

'Not beaten yet,' he answers and he sets off back up the path, gaining a ten-foot lead.

'I'm going to count to ten and I'll still beat you,' she shouts after him. They have about a mile to the summit.

'Coming, ready or not,' he hears over his shoulder. He has gained a good lead and he will need every foot of it.

Up the path they run. Up on the sunny summer morning. The walkers who follow later will enjoy the view, they will enjoy the stunning misty sights of Red Pike and Pillar, of Helvellyn and Scafell Pike. They will marvel at the spindly twisting, turning snake of the streams in the valley below reflecting in the sun. If they come late enough they will see the fells turn red in the sunset.

Ashley notices none of this. He wants to win. Even the fact that if he loses he has to hold her in his arms and teach her to dance doesn't matter. In his world, born and brought up in the East End, boys beat girls. Girls do music and clothes. Girls don't run. Girls don't run and certainly don't beat him. But, as he will discover in the coming months and years, what his instinct expects and his reality experiences are two very different things.

Up the hills they run. The two of them are locked in combat and he is losing. He can hear her getting closer. The path is drying out and he is slipping less, but so is she. Wandope has a vast flat top the size of a football pitch and the final run to the small cairn is all but flat.

He is panting now and heaving and, as the cairn comes into sight, she overtakes him. She runs with rhythm and elegance. She could be running in a sports day not to the top of a mountain. They have just climbed over 1,000 feet. He speeds up to try and retake the lead, but she just quickens her own pace. For the last two hundred yards, they are all but sprinting.

She is victorious. He is exhausted. Both stand at the cairn, chests heaving. Both are sweating, glistening, translucent in the morning sun. While she is out of breath, he is now bent double scrambling to get his breath back. The lactic acid from his final sprint has built up and he spits to remove the sharp taste out of his mouth.

Gradually he recovers. She is already composed.

'How? How come...?' is all he manages between breaths.

'How come I beat you? How come you are so good, is the real question. Fell-running is in my family. My dad is Cumbrian fell-running champion. My granddad was champion before him. I have been running since I could walk. I have won the juniors race for fell-running for the last two years. There are maybe ten people of my age who could give me a good race on these mountains and they all train, and have done since they were at primary school. Yet you gave me a good run for my money this morning. What's the story? When did you start running?'

'February,' he replies.

'Don't make me laugh,' she scoffs. 'Not February this year, no way.'

'February this year.'

'Well I never…if you haven't been training for years then you must have been born to run.'

They pause. They both eye each other, both savouring the view. She is taking in the fact that the mystery man she has been fascinated and tantalised by since he arrived just has got more intriguing.

'Now for my dancing lesson, Ash.'

'What, now? And I already told you, it's Ashley.'

'Yes of course, now. When better than now? The mountains are beautiful. The sun is rising. The day is young, and I want to learn to dance.'

So, on the top of Wandope, he teaches her to dance.

'Imagine we are lovers,' he starts.

'I am imagining, Ash,' she replies, smiling flirtatiously.

'It's Ashley. We are angry, we are cross. Each time I try to come close, you try to get away. That is our whole dance. Now you put your hand on my shoulder. I put my hand round your waist. We walk together like this with you going backwards. That's great. Now I walk backwards and we move together. Now you lean back as far as you can and I move as if to kiss you. If you are nimble you can throw your leg up in the air as well.

'Now you move away and just as you are about to be out of my reach I pull you back. I tug you back. We move back together and start again. Now we intertwine, your leg tugs me in.'

They stop for a moment and look into each other's eyes as they are meant to. They enjoy the moment. They are both warm and sweaty from the climb and they practise their dance.

She is a good pupil and, despite the lack of music, their dance still has style. They dance as he shows her the steps. When they finish, when they have held each other close and felt the warmth and heat of each other's bodies, when they have looked into each other's eyes and held their gaze again, when they have turned and moved their feet together and felt the sway of their bodies together, when the teacher has taught the pupil all that he knows, they stop and pause. What happens next, neither expected.

She leans towards him, and in a rare moment when she loses self-control, when her desire overcomes her need to have power, she kisses him on the lips. At first, he is shocked and it is just a peck. Then she comes back for more and he is ready. This time they kiss together. Their mouths open, their heads tilted, their tongues entwine and they pull toward each other. It is a moment of sheer pleasure where desire has triumphed over shyness. Neither of them will forget the magical excitement of their first kiss.

Jess regains her control.

'Thank you, Ash,' she says, as if he has just given her a chocolate bar. 'That's for giving me a hard race and a dancing lesson.'

And with that, she leaves him on the top of the mountain with the taste of her sweat and saliva in his mouth and a bulge in his trousers.

18: Consummation

Saturday 17th July

Since they were interrupted at the vicarage, Steve and Hazel have not met. They missed two weeks. She was on holiday and he was forbidden to go out on day release due to some minor indiscretion. Now, three weeks later, they are meeting again.

They text each other. She has told him to meet her at Catbells Terrace. She has a surprise in store. There is one house that everybody notices. It sits high on Catbells Terrace looking over the southern end of Derwentwater. It would never get planning permission today. It has stunning views over the lake and the mountains. It is a house that a thousand people have dreamed about owning, and Hazel is no different.

They greet each other. He has cycled from the farm. Kipper has run alongside him. She has parked in one of the lay-bys and is waiting with Rose by the car. She is determined that this time there will be no uncertainty when they meet, no awkward hands or fumbling. So, when they greet, she takes his hand and kisses him on the lips. He is taken aback but only momentarily and kisses her back. The dogs, as ever, sniff each other, and wag their tails.

'Come and see my surprise,' she whispers.

They leave the car and walk up a path towards the Terraces. The path takes them through the woods. The first tinges of high summer are beginning to show: the grass has lost its full green lustre and the tree leaves no longer look new enough to eat. The house is set back from the road three or four hundred yards. There are no neighbours, which she hopes means no interruptions.

At the door, she turns to him and says, 'This house has only just come to us. I got the keys yesterday and we aren't taking viewings till next week. I have the only set of keys, so we should be safe.'

'Safe for what?' he asks in mock innocence, 'Aren't we just going for a walk? That's what Kipper thinks.'

'Kipper and Rose can do their own thing for a bit. We have other plans.'

Again, they tie the dogs up outside so there are no dirty paws to give their game away.

She leads him straight up to the bedroom. Her heart is racing. His heart is racing. They have both dreamt about this moment. He has lain in his prison bed and fantasised about this moment more times than he can remember. She has thought about this moment in her daydreams repeatedly. Now it is here for real. She takes his hand and leads him up the stairs.

The view from the bedroom is beyond compare. They both pause briefly by the huge picture window but they are not here to see the view from the window. They are here to work out their lust.

'Now where were we before we were interrupted?'

'I think you were about to show me...'

She seizes his head in her hands and kisses him forcefully. He responds by picking her up and carries her to the bed and lays her gently on it. As he leans over she pulls him on top of her and takes his shirt off. He moves to pull her shirt off and they are both naked from the waist up. Then to his surprise she sits up and looks at him.

'I have to know something...'

'What?' he asks, and through his brain race a thousand things. Does she know about prison? Is she worrying about pregnancy or AIDS? The question that does come he did not expect.

'Does your wife know you are here?'

'My wife?' he asks incredulously.

'Yes, your wife. I have thought about this a lot. It's the only thing that makes sense. You get sent out on a Saturday to walk the dog. That's why you can only ever walk after 2 p.m. That's why you wouldn't give me your mobile number initially. It's why you are so rubbish at farming and so rubbish at knowing how to make a cup of tea. It's why I couldn't see your bedroom at the farm. You're married, you must be married or at least with a partner. There is no way somebody so gorgeous, so gentle, so handsome could be without a partner. All your weird behaviour can only make sense if you are married, so I need to know if she cares that you are with another woman.'

By now she can see the look on his face and in her panic she starts to gabble.

'How can you not be married? You must be married. I had it all figured out and, by the look on your face, she doesn't know you are with me. My hope was that the marriage was over but I can see that I am just a bit on the side for you. Oh God, I have been a fool. I knew it was too good to be true.'

She stops, wraps her arms around her head and starts wailing.

'I am not married,' he says quietly, reaching his hand out to touch her. 'I don't have a partner. There is no one else but you. The funny thing is that I thought you might be married.'

'You aren't married? Seriously! Really? Did you really mean

that there is no else but me? How can you not be married? Please promise me you aren't married and there is no one else. Are you gay?' she adds in desperation.

'I promise you there is no one else. I promise you I am not married. I am not gay. I promise I have only had eyes for you since the day we met.'

A look of relief comes over her. But then as her brain ticks she realises that she still has no idea who he is and the mystery of this man is still not explained.

'But then what is your secret?'

He moves to speak. He wants to tell her. He is about to tell her. He doesn't want the secret any more. But she stops him by putting her hand over his mouth.

'On second thoughts, I don't want to know. I have obsessed and worried that there was another woman, that there was somebody else and that you might not be the man of my dreams. But there is nobody else and anything you say now might spoil my perfect moment. So right here, right now, I want us to be together.'

So on this hot July day, she lies back. As the rest of the world moves on, as the sailboats on the lake flit back and forth, as the walkers toil up Catbells, as the launch leaves the jetty, as the scouts' canoes straggle across the bay, as the tourists eat their cream teas in Grange, they are together. On a hot July day, the rest of the world moves on, as the dogs patiently wait outside, heads on paws, while the young lovers, finally, consummate their desires.

Afterwards they lie together in the hazy, sleepy world of those precious moments after making love, each with their own thoughts. Eventually she turns to him and says, 'Did you really think I was married? What on earth would make you think I was married? Actually, don't answer that. I don't want anything to spoil this moment. You are all mine.'

One day, she knows that she will have to tell him about her secret: the imperfections of her body. One day he knows he will have to tell her about his secret: the wife and child he used to have. Today, they have felt the intimacy of their first precious moment together. One day they will have to know each other's secret, but not today. Not today. Looking out over this stunning view, the story yet to come cannot be allowed to spoil the here and now. For sadly, the worst is yet to come.

19: Behind Skiddaw

Saturday 7th August

Since the encounter on Wandope, Ashley has been in summer holiday mode. He has been off to Spain with his family. He has lain by the beach and swam in the sea. They went with his mum's sister and her family. A holiday week of card games, the banter with cousins, sea and sand and boredom

He and Jess are in a kind of limbo. They have texted each other a bit. What are they to each other? Are they girlfriend/boyfriend? Are they an item? He doesn't know. Does she know? What does she want?

He returns from holiday late on a Friday evening. Next morning at 9 a.m. he gets a text from Jess.

Ash, mt me Skiddaw Hse at 4 today for a run.

He texts back, *Sure – where Skiddaw Hse?*

She replies, *Find out. See you there.*

He is now flummoxed and slightly spooked. How does she know he is back? He didn't tell her. He looks on the map for Skiddaw House but can't find it. He looks it up in the guide book his mother keeps – still no joy. He wonders whether if he went to the top of Skiddaw all would become clear. It might, but not in time. It never occurs to him just to search for it online. What if he asked his mum? She might know but she would want to know why he wanted to know and he can't think of a good excuse. He is a teenager. She doesn't need to know and he doesn't want to tell her, so he continues his hunt for this run to a mystery destination.

By noon, he is beginning to panic. He has no idea where he is running to. And, despite her bossy manner, he has the hots for her as much as ever. He wants their relationship to be…to be real.

At last, inspiration, he remembers Wainwright. His mother has the complete set. He rarely looks at them. They are some kind of weird trophy walking book, but Wainwright makes detailed maps of all sorts of places. He looks at the books and selects 'Northern Fells'. At last he finds the information he been searching for.

Skiddaw House is an isolated hostel round the back of Skiddaw. He has to get the way up from Latrigg. It's miles away and there is no easy way to get there. She is testing him. The run starts in the middle of nowhere – rather than ends in the middle of nowhere, but knowing her, that might happen as well. Or perhaps she is just playing hard to get.

At 3 p.m. he sets off on his bicycle. He tells his mum he is going for a bike ride. He parks his bike on the top of Latrigg and chains it to the fence in the Gale Road Car Park.

Time is tight but not too bad. Its 3.20 p.m. when he sets off from the car park. The beginning of the run from Gale Road goes well. The path is wide and easy, cutting behind the Celtic cross of the Shepherd's memorial. He is too far along the path when he discovers that the path is well used by mountain bikers coming the other way, and he might have been able to bike most of the way.

It is mountain bikes that nearly put an end to getting to Skiddaw House at all. After he has been walking for twenty minutes he reaches a narrow stretch of the path with a steep slope of heather and bracken stretching down to the river in the valley bottom. As he navigates one of the numerous muddy puddles created by a stream crossing the path, three mountain bikers come shooting around a corner ahead.

He steps to one side to let them pass, standing on a small dry tuft just where a stream disappears over the edge. The biker passes closer the others and he instinctively move back further and he foot slips on the wet edge. He falls into thin air and lands in the mud six feet below. The momentum carries him another twenty feet and his comes to a halt as his shins hit a rock on the slope just to the edge of the stream.

He sits up and examines his legs, and feels for other bumps and bruises. There is a nasty graze on one elbow and some scrapes on his legs. He's wet and streaked with mud. He stands up and nothing gives way. He scrambles back up to the path and watching carefully for bikes, finds a dry section and hauls himself back up onto the path.

He pauses for a moment, trying to decide whether to go on. But nothing hurts too much, so he sets off walking in the direction of Skiddaw House.

He is now almost late, but the route from his river crossing to Skiddaw House is not too far. As Skiddaw House comes into view, he can see she's not there. He is part relieved and part bewildered. Did he misunderstand where she meant? Is there another Skiddaw House? He arrives at 4.07 p.m. by his watch. He checks the text she sent him. He checks she meant today. He checks that she said 'Skiddaw House'. He wonders if there is some meaning of 'hse' he has not thought of.

After ten minutes of waiting he texts her, 'Where u?' But there is no signal. He waits a few minutes more and then starts to jog home, subdued and irritated.

A voice from behind him calls, 'Ash, am I not worth waiting for?'

He turns and Jess is standing on the path behind him.

'Oh, what happened to you?' she adds, trying to suppress a smile, seeing his mud-splattered figure and scraped legs.

'It's Ashley,' he interrupts. 'Where have you been? I half killed myself to get here on time. I have smashed my legs and have a sore bum and it turns out I could have walked here at a snail's pace.'

'I'm sorry. It took me longer to get here than I thought it would.'

She is lying. He knows she is lying. She knows he knows she is lying. But she can see he is angry so, instead of the teasing which she had intended, she just backs off. Had he been like the buzzard at the top of the Scots Pine behind Skiddaw House he would have seen her arrive early and wait for him hiding at a distance. He would have seen her pleased and puffed up that he arrived so dishevelled and that she was worth waiting for. She needs to be in control. She cannot let him (yet) make the moves, because what if he doesn't? What if she left him to kiss her and he didn't? Jess wants to stay in control, and makes the next move.

'I am sorry, Ash. Please forgive me.'

She moves to hug him. He is still angry. She puts her arms around him and looks at his face. She kisses him and repeats her apology. He tries to stay angry, but he has no chance, because slowly, like an ice cream left in the sun, he melts. She kisses him on the lips and he halfheartedly returns the kiss.

'Run away with me,' she appeals and pauses. He looks at her with amazement. 'Just to the end of the valley,' she adds, with a coy smile.

'Jess, I am not your plaything. You can't just mess me around.' He pushes her away and looks at her. 'And you certainly can't beat me to the end of the valley. Goodbye.' And with that he runs off towards Mosedale with a smile on his face.

'You bugger,' she cries after him, and the race is on.

The Mosedale Valley is a hidden valley. Away from the crowds who toil up Skiddaw and Blencathra, away from cars and roads, away from civilisation. It is surrounded on four sides by mountains. There are routes and paths in and out but it is far from the madding crowd. It is a favourite of cyclists and runners. Down the middle runs a river and many passing runners have cooled down with the cold fresh water flowing over stones that have been carved and ground and bashed and buffeted by the waters over thousands of years. Their shapes perfect as formed by nature. The observant can see the lizard hugging the sun on rocks and the wheatear and the chiffchaff perching on the rusting fences and the river reeds.

The wannabe lovers set off, down the valley with Skiddaw and the sun at their backs on this summer evening. The start of the route is flat and easy. Their pace is effortless. They are both determined to win. They pass the round stone sheep pens built generations ago by the toil of sweating shepherds. They pass cyclists coming up the valley. They are both in their element.

Watch them as runners. He is the new boy to this and she the latest in a long line of fell-runners, but together they are beautiful. They are running with life before them. They will both win prizes for their speed and agility. And, more and more, they will both discover that they were born to run, born for that effortless stamina, born with the wiry physique of people who can run at speed for hours. Together, they are beautiful.

She is still behind him. He has been training. On holiday, he didn't spend all his time with his cousins. He ran on the beach every day, most days twice a day, at least five miles every time. His mother watched and wondered. She watched as her son, her son who barely walked to school, her son who loved his PlayStation and his bus rides in London, now pounds the miles relentlessly. Something had got into him since they moved. She couldn't identify the change but she was thrilled. Soon it will lead her son to confront her as he has never done before and, when he does, she will be forced to confess to a secret that she has kept since he was born. But that is not today, and for now, Ashley's mother is pleased that her son is running.

He is pleased that he has run too. He is keeping better pace than before. Jess is not so pleased. She decides to change her tactics.

'Let's take a break,' she calls from behind him.

'No tricks?' he replies.

'No tricks, I promise.'

He stops running moments later by a small stream. They stand, their chests heaving. They are both sweating. She sits on a rock.

'Did you bring a drink?' she asks.

'Yes, but it's almost all gone.'

'Mine too.'

'Even though you arrived late, heh?'

She ignores this jibe.

'We can fill up from this stream. There are only dead sheep above here,' she says with a smile. They both fill their water bottles and drink deeply.

He fills his water bottle again.

'Stand here. Look towards Skiddaw and shut your eyes.'

'You must be kidding. You'll run off. I'm no fool.'

'I won't run off and I won't lay a finger on you. Promise.'

She shuts her eyes and faces Skiddaw and feels the warmth of the sun. As she does so, he stands behind her and takes first his and then her bottle, freshly filled with the icy water, and tips it over her. She screams. She screams with the cold. She screams with rage and turns to face him.

'I am cooling you down,' he pleads. 'Let me finish and then you can do it to me.'

The water has soaked her hair. It has run down her shirt which is now clinging to her figure. Her shirt is tight against her rounded breasts which are just in front of him. He wants to reach out and touch them.

'Cooler now?' She looks at him with a mixture of shock, desire, delight and retribution in her eyes.

'Your turn. Look away while I refill.' He stands patiently, savouring this relationship foreplay.

She pours the water over his head and his shoulders. He too gasps with the cold. He squeals as she pours it down his back. And then, when she demands a refill as he 'is bigger', he meekly agrees. She exacts her revenge by pulling open the top of his shorts and pouring the last of the water in. He reaches out and just catches her. He pulls her to him and they kiss, the water squelching in their shoes.

'Where now?' he asks.

'Well, I thought we might have a better race going up to Carrock Fell and then along the ridge and down in Mungrisdale.'

'You mean you think you might beat me that way?' He is right to be suspicious.

'I just want to expand your horizons, but now you mention it, I had better lead.'

They set off. A few hundred yards further on, she peels off the valley bottom path and takes a narrow path, high with bracken and then heather which heads up towards the ridge. She has been canny. It is harder for him to overtake here, so he bides his time and follows in her footsteps.

At the ridge she pauses. They have climbed over 300 feet in a little over twenty minutes. They can now see the whole of the Mosedale Valley. It is a vast 'L' shape. To the east, the farms are sheltered in the lee of the mountains from the winter storms and to the south and west they can see the way they have come. Before them are three more miles of ridge. There are stunning views in all directions. They can see as far as the Pennines twenty miles away and Hesket Newmarket snuggled in under the mountain to the north.

Still they run.

Another twenty minutes, and they are close to the edge of the escarpment. There is nothing before them but space and the path down. As any fell-runner knows going up mountains is only one test of running, coming down is the other.

Each step going down is a test of tendons and joints. Each step going down is an opportunity to slip or lose a footing and fall. And, yes, Jess was right. He has not the skill or experience to descend the mountain with speed.

And as she descends the escarpment, he slows down and she speeds up. He is nervous where she is sure-footed. She beats him easily to the bottom of the slope and the narrow road that snakes around the fells. By the time he reaches the bottom she is flat out on the grass by the side of the road. She is loathed to admit it but she is nearly as knackered as he is.

'You got here at last, Ash,' she says as he arrives.

'I'll beat you. I'll beat you one day. Have no fear. And then you can promise to call me Ashley.'

'What's wrong with being called Ash?' she asks, without wanting an answer. 'I don't have any fear that you'll beat me. I think all that hair slows you down. Were you walking down the last bit? To be honest…aaaaah.'

He sits *on* her, legs astride her chest.

'I think you are rude,' he tells her. He is right of course. It's much easier to be rude, and to tease, than it is to praise and tell him what she really feels. If she tells him that she is infatuated too and he fills her thoughts, he might not return the praise and then she is vulnerable. So he has sat on her chest. They are still like two fighting birds, lovebirds, even, circling, strutting, feathers puffed, and proud; neither wants to show any weakness.

'What are you doing? Get off me,' she protests, hoping he'll do no such thing.

'I am going to teach you a lesson.' He holds her hands above her head and leans down and kisses her. She makes a minor effort to resist. But soon their tongues are fighting, wrestling, wet and exploring.

'I like your lessons. I like them very much,' she whispers in a tone that is conciliatory.

'You are a good pupil,' he grins. 'How are we getting back?'

'Let's run to the main road, and when the bus comes, we can catch it. Now you can get off my chest.'

They walk for the first few hundred yards, not quite brave enough to hold hands. They meet the ponies of Mungrisdale, a collection of short-legged and stroppy ponies that live half-wild in the open spaces this side of the mountains. She goes to pet one and it responds but only because it is used to begging for food.

He uses his mobile to take a picture. She protests and demands to take one of him with his phone. They look at them and smile. He holds out the phone and takes a photo of both of them. They hold each other tightly.

Moments later, the walkers' bus arrives and they flag it down.

It is empty except for them and one solitary walker who sits at the front. Like primary school children, they scamper to the back row and then, with all the seats to choose from, they sit one row from the back.

The bus stops and starts. He stares out the window. She leans her head on his shoulder. They are each left with their own thoughts. They are still afraid to hold hands, to make that move from lust to affection. His shoulder is stiff as she leans against it. He puts his arm round her shoulder and pulls her in close. She responds by reaching across and holding his hand. Their fingers interlock. They both look out of the window, saying nothing, as if their fingers are not their own. She squeezes his hand. He squeezes her back. She flits her eyes up to try and catch his expression, but fails. He is still looking out the window. If she had moved her head up she would have seen that his eyes are shining.

It is nearly 8 p.m. by the time the bus reaches Booths store in Keswick.

The next morning, he walks up to the Gale Road Car Park and retrieves his bicycle, left behind, a casualty of the awkwardness of new love.

20. Ospreys and St Bega's

Monday 23rd August

Over the next few weeks of the summer holidays, as the start of term approaches, Ashley and Jess see more of each other. They are closer now, as their defences come down and their closeness increases.

On a late August evening Jess sends him a text.

Tonight. Scarness. 7pm. Where the ospreys feed. Look for the bench.

He has never been to Bassenthwaite, or the small bay on the east side, Scarness. It just beyond Mirehouse, a magnificent old stately home.

He forms a plan to exact his revenge for the way Jess played with him at Skiddaw House. He gets to Scarness an hour beforehand. He finds a clear patch of grass out of sight, next to the small bay which is surrounded by reeds. He spots the bench on the far side of the bay in a clearing in the reeds. He guesses she will come to the bench first. The grass is long and the insects are out in force on this warm August evening. He had not calculated on this and before long the midges have found him and are having their evening meal.

By the time she arrives fashionably late, at 7.45 p.m., he has endured over an hour and a half of the insects. On his arms alone he has counted over fifty bright red weals where the bites have come up. He can feel them on his face.

She is clad in her tight lycra jogging pants and an old white T-shirt which hangs over her breasts. She looks out for him, figuring that he should be there by now.

As he watches, she pushes up her shirt high up to let her tummy catch the sun. She stretches her leg out to bask a bit more, and turns her face to the warm rays. From his hiding place, he makes a noise like what he thinks should be a duck. She sits upright looking for the source of the noise. He makes the noise twice more and then doubles back so as to appear from the right direction. When he appears, she throws her arms around him and kisses him, and then pulls back.

'Are you all right?' she says, looking at his face. 'You look like you've been bitten to pieces! Look at your arms – what happened? Oh Ash, why are you late?'

'I'm fine,' he lies, trying to sound authoritative. 'Why are you late?

'*Me,* late. You came after me. How would you know?' She looks at him suspiciously. 'You wouldn't have come early to try and ambush me, would you? You are so gorgeous.'

'No no, of course not. I…'

He is stumped and realises that his plan has failed because of midge bites and his clumsy lies. Sensing his awkwardness, she puts her fingers to his lips to silence him.

'No fighting today. I have some things to show you. Come sit on the bench. The ospreys feed around now as the fish rise. Oh, you might like this mosquito repellent. It good for midges too. I always have some at this time of year. I thought you would know,' she adds with a teasing smile.

They wait and he tries to sit still and not scratch his bites. She holds his hand against the lycra of her thighs, which distracts him from the bites, temporarily.

As they sit she points out the form of an osprey high above the lake.

'We need to be very still and very quiet and hope they come to feed close by,' she whispers in his ear.

After fifteen minutes their patience is rewarded. Just as he thinks he can resist the temptation to scratch no longer, there is a rush of air overhead, a flash of white belly and brown wings as an osprey plunges into the bay fifty metres ahead of them. Moments later, it emerges with a fish in its talons, loses its grip with one claw, and as the fish struggles, the osprey drops the fish. The bird turns instantly and dives back in the water to re-catch its floundering prey. Successful this time, the raptor flies off to the left, as their two heads turn to watch.

'Wow,' he breathes.

'Come, I have something else I want to show you.'

She takes his hand and they walk down a tiny path through the reeds, along the water's edge. As the sun begins to set, they walk past a hay meadow and they emerge onto a lane. A hundred yards along the lane they reach a kissing gate she pauses and whispers '*kissing* gate', and he obliges. After a few hundred yards of walking, they reach another gate and she points. He exclaims, part in wonder, and part because he knows that is what she wants.

It is a ship, an island, an oasis, a mirage in the middle of the field half a mile away: a small church surrounded by a small graveyard and a stone wall in the middle of a field where sheep and cows are grazing.

'St Bega's,' she says her voice almost a whisper, 'the church of St Bega's. Apparently, it was built in memory of an Irish nun who came over in the seventh century. I love it and the way it is just so out of place. Inside it's beautiful. The setting is perfect.'

They walk towards the church with Mirehouse behind it

'As a little girl, I came down here once, and there was a wedding going on. I had never seen a wedding before. The cars were all parked on the grass. I watched as the bride arrived in a Rolls Royce. As she got out, I nearly fainted with excitement. She was so beautiful in her long white dress. There was a band playing and all these people were dressed in their smartest clothes. I waited outside as the service went on and afterwards they came outside to eat strawberries and drink champagne at the lakeside. I just watched in awe. It was a perfect day in a perfect setting.'

She stops talking. She wants to tell him the dreams she had when she was a little girl. How she imagined herself getting married like the woman she watched as a child. She dreams about her perfect day, with her perfect man in her perfect setting. She is wise enough not to have finished her story. Whatever her feelings for this boy, this man whose hand she is holding, she does not want to alarm him. So she keeps her thoughts to herself – for now.

At the church yard they go in through the gate. The graveyard has a high wall surrounding it. There are graves from 200 and 300 years ago, some with vast table tops supported by four deep red stone pillars. There is a large yew tree which looks like it has been here hundreds of years.

Inside the church, the smell is the first thing he notices. It's the smell of polish and pews, of congregations and hymn books, the smell of history and age. He breathes in deeply. She watches him out of the corner of her eye, willing him to love this place, aching that he feels the same kind of things that she feels.

He looks around. He remembers the church that he went into on his last day at school down south. While that was grand and monumental, it was also cold and characterless. This church feels like the personalities, the souls, the grime of church-goers, the toil of vicars, have rubbed off on the pews and the pulpit. This church has etched in it the Sunday services for a community of farmers on their day of rest as they prayed for better weather, no snow at lambing time, and that their meagre vegetable plots would grow.

So, while Jess dreams of marriage, Ashley imagines the long line of men and their womenfolk down the generations. He sees the large egg-timer on the wall. He looks at it in amazement. A relic of an age before watches and clocks, when the sermon must be timed before the congregation became restless.

He goes outside to explore the churchyard and to find somewhere to pee, and leaves her inside. He tells her he'll be outside and leaves the door open.

After about six paces, he has a sudden thought and grins. He pees outside the wall of the churchyard and then leans back over the wall at right angles to the door of the church so she just can't see him when she comes out. There he makes his duck noise again.

Jess emerges from the church, her face rich with withering contempt at his attempt to wind her up. She looks around and then spots him. He is grinning from ear to ear.

'Is something the matter?' he says.

'You think you are so funny, don't you? You were spying on me, were you? You thought you would be so clever. Now I know what the bites are from. You lay in wait for me, and the bugs had a feast. You tried to trick me. Ha. Well, you are very lucky that you are the other side of that wall.'

'Why would that be? You can't catch me, you are carrying a few too many pounds.'

'A few too many pounds? I am going to get you…Run! Run now! Run for your life!'

He skips away backwards towards the lake, still laughing. To his surprise, she leaps, with one hand on the top of the wall, over the churchyard wall in a single bound.

Momentarily his face falls.

'Run, Ash! Run. Because when I get you! When I get you...!'

She chases him and he runs to the lake as quickly as he can, but giggling, laughing at his own hilarity, not really minding if he is caught. As he reaches the lakeside, she catches him. She holds him by the wrist.

'You need to be punished. Lie down.'

He looks at her with a look of pity as if she is mad to think he would lie down voluntarily.

'LIE DOWN,' she says with a voice full of authority.

'No way. No way. Why should I lie down? You took me for a ride at Skiddaw House and I have got my own back here. Now we are quits.'

'That was getting your own back!' she exclaims, and adds with mock surprise, 'I took you for a ride at Skiddaw House? Well I never. I merely waited to make sure you would show up. It's not good for a girl to be left loitering for a boy. Now, lie down so I can punish you. You need to feel those extra pounds.'

He shakes his head slowly, while keeping his eyes firmly fixed on hers. They are both enjoying this contact, both enjoying the excuse to not take their eyes off each other. Just as he thinks he has got the upper hand, she moves her left foot in front of him, swings her hips into his middle, pulls down hard with her right arm on his left, and he is on his back on the grass. In a flash, she sits across his chest and pins his arms to his sides with her kneeling legs.

'Did I tell you I do judo at school?' she enquires with a mocking tone. 'Now, as punishment, you have a choice. You can either choose a forfeit today or a forfeit on a later one.'

'Don't I get to know the two forfeits?'

'Oh, I don't know, let me check,' she says. Then, mimicking him, she continues, 'Porky' Jess says "no". Porky Jess says, "I should hit you over the head with a shovel." That's all the information you get. Today or not today.'

'Not today, then. There'll be more time for snogging today. I'll take my punishment another day.'

'Snogging,' she snorts, 'snogging. In your dreams. Your punishment is that you have to race in the UK fell-running championships at the end of October. This year, they are taking place in Borrowdale. Locals under eighteen are allowed three places, but at the moment there are only two places taken, so I thought you could take the third place in the men's race.'

'Sounds good to me. Does that mean I can beat you in a race?'

She lifts herself off him and stands up, deliberately not answering his question.

'Don't think you'll *ever* beat me in a race, and don't think you can ever outwit me. You should treasure me more,' she says in a wounded tone, while brushing off the grass and leaves that have stuck to her. 'So you'll race then?'

'Yes, I'll race,' he concedes.

'Good. I thought I might have to twist your arm to get you to race, but you gave in quite easily.'

She turns and walks back the way they came. The sun is now just going down over the lake. And, looking back over her shoulder, it is her turn to adopt an impish grin –

'I'm running, of course, but in your race both my older brothers are competing. Sorry, didn't I tell you that? I've told them how good you are, so they are keen to see whether you can stand up against them.'

He looks in astonishment at her as she walks away.

21: Walking with the past

Saturday 4th September

The shepherdess has asked both Steve and Ashley to help her with the annual ritual of separating lambs from their mothers, and trimming the ewes. Her Saturday man and Sunday boy will be meeting for the first time. They both now feel a sense of belonging, of ownership, attachment to Joyce, to her farm, to these sheep.

They are aware of each other through what Joyce has told them. Joyce is careful not to let on about Steve and prison. Even so, both are nervous and awkward with each other.

'Hi.'

'Hi.'

'I'm Ashley.'

'I'm Steve. I have heard about your running. You help on Sundays, don't you?'

'Yeah. You do Saturday, don't you?'

'Yeah. Nice to meet you.'

'And you.'

They exchange few words the whole time they help together. Anybody but a teenage boy might have asked what Steve does the rest of the week.

Once the lambs are separated, Ashley departs and leaves Joyce and Steve to help with foot-trimming.

Joyce regularly brings in all her ewes to check their feet, teeth and general condition. However, getting to a sheep's feet is not easy. They are not like horses, which usually stand placidly while the blacksmith does his work. The only way to trim a sheep's feet is to turn it on its back and rest it upright between a strong pair of legs so it can't get a grip on the ground to struggle or move.

It's a job that can be done solo, but it is more back-breaking leaning over to trim feet with a ewe wedged between your knees. The ewes mill about in the yard, their lambs now in another field and all but forgotten. Steve pushes them into a circular pen where one gate lets them in from the yard and on the other side a panel can be opened to act as an exit. Three or four ewes are pushed in so they can be checked and feet-trimmed by Joyce sitting on a stool.

Steve catches a ewe and then wrestles it over by pulling its head back and leaning down to find a leg and pulls it off balance. With the local Herdwicks and Swaledales this can be relatively easy as they are lighter. Joyce's heavier, not to mention meatier Suffolks are altogether harder. Ewe by ewe, he works to secure each against his knees.

Joyce then moves in to do the trimming. She has a squat old plastic beer crate that she sits on to examine and work. As she works they chat. Joyce always happy to ask the questions as they occur to her.

'What will you do when you get out?'

'Get out?' Steve queries, not quite believing the question she is asking.

'You know, from prison.'

'Like today with you, you mean.'

'No!' she retorts scornfully, not realising that this might be a sensitive issue. 'Not like today, but for good. What will you do? Where will you go?

'Wow. That's a big question. I haven't thought much about it.'

Joyce looks up at him, disbelieving.

'I haven't!' he protests.

'Are you ready to leave prison?' she asks. 'Oh, this one's feet are bad. I think there is some foot rot in these front two. Can you pass me the paring knife? If I do the first few trims, perhaps, you can try and cut some of the rotten area with the knife.'

A minute or so later, the ewe's foot is trimmed and an area of foot rot is exposed up the side. Joyce takes the anti-biotic purple spray and warns Steve to turn away so they don't inhale the spray, and moves onto the next foot. Steve had hoped she might have forgotten her question, but she hasn't.

'Well, are you?'

'Most weeks, I would say...I don't know.' His voice tails off. He comes back with renewed energy as he realises there is no else he can reveal these feelings to.

'I am still haunted by Zoe, I realise. By the thought of what might have been. I think about her a lot. She comes to me in my dreams – actually, I should probably call them nightmares. Not that anything bad necessarily happens. It's more of a haunting. It gets worse around her birthday, knowing I can't see her...should I just forget about her? Should I have moved on? I know that you say that prison has been good for me, but if I was out of prison I would have daily life to distract me. In prison, there is too much time to think. It's so easy to dwell on things.'

'This one is done; let her go gently with those bad feet. It might be worth keeping her in overnight while her front two feet dry out a bit. Catch the next one for me. What happens when you dwell on her?'

149

Steve catches and turns another ewe and as Joyce positions her stool next to the ewe's feet, he starts again.

'I imagine what she would be doing. What she would be like. I see something in the news about children of the right age and it gets me thinking. Dwelling. Mourning. One of the early walks back in May with the dogs…'

He pauses, as the emotion chokes him, and Joyce, too, pauses and looks up. He starts again.

'One of the early walks with the dogs, I walk past a group of about six kids. It's a warm May afternoon. As I go up the mountain, they are resting and having a snack. Three boys and three girls. When we go past, Kipper can see that they have food and stops to beg.

'Can I give your dog a treat, mister?' one of them asks.

'So we stop to talk. I ask them, "What are you all doing up here on the mountain?" Duke of Edinburgh award, they tell me. I'd never heard of it. They have to do a walk and overnight camp, apparently. There are three other groups from their school doing other walks out at the same time. They are chatty and tell me about how they are finding it.

'One of the girls is the friendliest and likes Kipper the best. And then it hits me. It hits me. This girl, this smiley, sweet, charming, pretty girl is probably about the same age as Zoe. I should have stopped the conversation right then. I don't. You see, Joyce, up till then, every bit of thinking I have been doing about what she would be like was in my head. There are no real girls of that age in prison. They are all in my head. Now there is one in front of me. A living version of what till now has been in my imagination. I can't help myself, and so I ask them what age they are. Year 9, they say. My blank face must tell them this meant nothing to me.'

He sighs. He has needed to tell this story. He can't afford to talk to the prison shrink, in case it rocks the boat on his release date. Who else is there to talk to in his life except Joyce? Not Hazel, who knows nothing about any of this.

'The chatty girl tells me she has just turned fourteen. So then she is Zoe. Every curl of hair, every freckle, every mannerism, every word is my daughter. There in front of me. And I can't get that thought out of my head. So I start to well up. I just have crazy thoughts. Maybe this is Zoe. Is that the scar on her forehead where she hit the table? I meet one girl of about the right age and in seconds I am a mess.

'Her companions move to leave but she can see that I have changed. "You've gone white, Mister," she says.

'I'm sorry,' I whisper, 'but you remind me of somebody I once knew.'

'Neither of us know what to say. Her companions have moved away and are telling her to "come on"'. She moves to leave and then I ask her.'

He hesitates again. Joyce looks up to see the tears in his eyes.

'And then I ask her if I can give her a kiss. The girl looks shocked and backs away. It was stupid. If the prison found out, I would be set back years. Her companions can see I have said something. One of the boys starts to come back and then he calls out...he calls out...'

Steve voice trails off. His voice is full of tears. In a whisper, he finishes his story.

'The boy calls out to the girl, "Come on Zoe, we need to get going."

'I swear the pain of that could have been a real dagger. My throat constricts and my legs give way, and I collapse in the path. The girl looks at me, having no comprehension of what has just happened. She can see she has had some effect on me. "I'm sorry. I have to go," she says, her eyes of full of bewildered concern as she backs off down the path.'

His tears drip onto the belly of the ewe and become small clear patches on the floor of the yard amongst the sheep shit and the dirt. Joyce has stopped her work as his story finished. To begin with, there is silence, which Joyce finally breaks.

'What does Hazel know, Steve?'

Steve looks at her with alarm.

'She knows nothing, Joyce,' he replies eventually, eyes staring at the floor.

'She needs to know it all, Steve. She needs to know what you feel. She needs to know what you've done. What does she think you do? Does she still think you are a farmer? Surely not.'

'Why do you say all this now?'

'Because when I thought what you had done was part of the past, like a one-night stand that you never confessed to, it was one thing. What you have just told me makes it clear that it is also part of you, now. And if you want your relationship with Hazel to flourish, you can't have a secret of that size without it having an impact.'

'I know you are right. But telling her is not that easy.'

'And the longer you leave it the harder it will get. There, that's this one finished. We have done about twenty ewes today, which isn't too bad. The rest will have to wait for another day.'

She stands up and is back nearly at his eye level. She looks at him, unblinking.

'You need to tell her, Steve. You need to tell her.'

22: Going nowhere

Saturday 18th September

Steve and Hazel still meet, still walk, still have sex, and the dogs still wait patiently by the front doors of many houses. There is a routine to their meetings. They are working out their desires on each other. For now, this routine will stand.

After his conversation with Joyce, Steve knows he has to say something. But he daren't. And so they walk, have sex, and try to pretend everything is all right.

The pretence is gone. No longer does he cycle with a dog under one arm or pretend to meet her by chance on the fells. They meet in particular places. She picks him up in the car from the farm. They don't ask too many questions, just in case they reach the territory that neither wants to explore.

So is it to be a house on Lonsties, or a flat in Blencathra Street? They visit each of them and perform their weekly ritual. Variety is not talk, but place. They find secluded spots in the fells among the bracken. They still talk. They talk about the fells, about the birds, about the world, about the books they have read and anything and everything except themselves. They just don't talk about feelings or their respective secrets. They are like double agents. Expunging from their minds the things they cannot talk about. The topics they cannot cross. If you never want to be disappointed, never ask a question which may have the answer you don't want to hear.

They have found a few favourite places. One is the old run-down house on the back route to Barrow. Here, they have found a little sheltered spot where the roof has not quite fallen down, and even when it's raining they go through their sterile routine. Quite frankly, it's all a bit grubby.

Here they are on a late September afternoon. The first colours are just beginning to turn. The schools have gone back and the hillsides are quiet. The afternoon is warm and for those who venture out, the rewards are great.

On the back route to Barrow, there is a path. Once it might have been a route to a house, but the house has now fallen down. The trees have grown large. They provide shade on hot summer days. One day, this house will be majestic again, perhaps lived in by a farmer and his young family, who will enjoy the landscape from their windows. But for now, the ruins remain, and they are there lying on a blanket. His trousers are around his ankles. His coat is hitched up. She is all but hidden from view. This is a private act, open to the skies.

Gemma has run ahead of her parents. Aged seven, she has always been fascinated by the run-down house. Whenever she walks past on the Saturday afternoon walk with her family, her imagination is fired up. She imagines this is her castle. She is the princess. So she runs ahead because she knows her parents don't like her playing around the house. She creeps through the fence. She stands where the front door should be. There are two people in her house. She is amazed and indignant. She cannot work out what they are doing. She can only see a pair of white globes rise and fall, so she asks.

Her parents have always encouraged her to ask questions.

'What are you doing?'

Movement stops, but no one answers her.

'Excuse me, what are you doing?' She actually means, *what are you doing in my house where I dream of being a princess.*

A face appears. Two faces appear. Gemma is shocked to see there is a woman there as well.

'Are you all right? This house is my castle, you know, and when I grow up, I am going to be a princess and live in it.'

'We're fine. Thank you. My friend here was just, well she was needing...' He struggles for words.

'I have got an itch,' Hazel whispers in his ear.

Steve finishes his sentence. '...she had an itch, so we needed to find somewhere sheltered so I could scratch her itch.'

Our lovers dare not move. They dare not let the little girl see any more.

'It must be a big itch if you are doing it with your whole bodies,' Gemma replies matter of factly.

'Yes, it was a big itch that my friend had.'

At that point they are rescued.

'Gemma, where are you? Gemma. Gemma.' Her parents have noticed she has run ahead but is nowhere to be seen.

'I've got to go,' says Gemma. 'It was very nice to meet you.' And with that, she runs off.

They both collapse in nervous laughter.

'An itch indeed.'

'It was your idea.'

'Well, you come up with a better one next time.'

They try to return to their itching, but the moment has gone. Today, even the desire has gone flat. Words are the only things that can bring them back together, but the words aren't coming.

23: Farewell, my friend

Thursday 7th October

The dog's eyebrows twitch, moving from side to side with her eyes as she studies her mistress' face. Sitting in her armchair, Joyce is holding Queenie's head in her hands. She is leaning forward in her chair, her eyes searching the dog's face.

'How could I miss it? How could I miss your lump, Queenie? Now I can see it. Now the vet has told me, I can see it. I can see that great fucking lump pushing your eyeball out. Distorting your face. But I missed it. I missed it. I've let you down. All these years you've been here by my side. Us two lonely girls and the eunuch boy. But we've been the girls. You and me. You and me.'

As she talks, a drip of blood trickles down the dog's nose and before Queenie's tongue can lick it, it drips on the floor. Joyce begins a quiet ululating sob. Her breaths come in rasps. Kipper and Queenie stare at their owner, concerned and bewildered. She starts again. Her voice soft and trembling.

'Do you remember…do you remember when you first arrived, just after I started here? We were both as hopeless as each other. You, the runt of the litter. No good for proper sheep work, that shepherd said. Too slow. Too stupid. But you were perfect for me.

Us two rejects, wallowing together in our stupidity. Too proud to change our minds. Exiled into the cold wastes of hill farming.'

She pauses again, blows her nose and wipes her tears. After years alone, talking to her dogs is quite normal for Joyce. She sometimes thinks if she didn't have her dogs to talk to, she would go quite mad.

'That first time we tried herding the ewes. Ohh, how little did I know. I was meant to lead you, and you ended up leading me. I still remember our useless effort – well, my useless effort, on that first morning. The ewes, all new and skittish and stubborn. How was I to know that ewes need to get used to a dog before they can be easily herded? Me sending you up one side and getting my 'cum by' and 'cum ere' muddled up. And the way you kept looking back with this look on your face saying *are you sure you know what you are doing?*

'They say that a shepherd's job is to harness the killing instinct with their dog. It was never like that with you, was it? Harnessing the instincts of a great big softie more like, with you. When that big sheep stopped on that first day, halfway round the field, and wouldn't move and just looked at you, you looked at me and I shouted at you, and she only moved when I walked across the field to shoo her as well. She was number 38, of course. If there were three lonely girls, she could be the third perhaps.'

Joyce lets go of Queenie's head, and with the eyes of both dogs watching her, she crosses the room and flicks the kettle on.

'All these tears have made me thirsty,' she says, and pauses, waiting for the kettle. Then she turns back to Queenie and, forcing the words out, starts again.

'On...on...on Saturday,' and here her voice cracks, 'we're taking you, me and Steve, we're taking you to the vet, you see, my Queenie. It's not your fault. Behind that bulging eye and head is a tumour. It's pushing against your brain. That's why you had that fit last week. Yelping in pain you were, and thrashing about. The vet said you haven't got long, a week or two. I don't want you to suffer. Not after how good we have been together. After that first day, we got better and better, didn't we? So the lovely vet will give you something to help you sleep and we will bring you back here for the last time. Me and Steve are taking you. He will be my rock on Saturday. We will bury you up in the top field, so you look over your flock for always.

'I am sorry, Queenie. I am *so* sorry. You have been my rock all these years. Not fickle and grumpy like people, not like my family. You don't peddle forgiveness like a weapon. You just love. And you have loved me and I have loved you.'

She moves back to her armchair, puts the cup of tea down and takes Queenie's head back in her hands, and leans her forehead against the top of Queenie's head. She breathes in the smell of dog. The warmth of her soft head and ears. The murmur of her quiet breath. She strokes with her thumb the bulge in Queenie's skull where the tumour has pushed it outwards.

'Thank you. You have been a friend like no else could have been.'

And her words are lost in the rasping sobs of her despair.

Saturday 9th October

The vet is a slim, smiley young woman. The brightest in her class at school. An animal lover for as long as she can remember. She worked hard at vet school. She learnt about more diseases, more animals, more conditions, and more illnesses than any doctor ever does. Despite her size, she has had to calve a pregnant cow, treat mastitis in sheep, and lameness in a horse. However, the farmers prefer male vets and ones with the years of untaught experience of sheep and cattle farming, not just what can be learnt in books.

So this female vet tends to be landed with the small animal work. The cats and dogs and small furries. So on an October Saturday morning she greets an oddball couple. An older lady with greying hair, a lined face and the worn-out clothes of a farm life. The man is harder to place. Probably in his thirties, but with a face lined with hardship. In tow is an old collie dog, nervous and hugging the walls in this unfamiliar place.

Before the vet can say a word the woman starts.

'She needs to be put to sleep.' Steve lifts her on the table.

The vet is taken aback. No small talk, just a request to kill this dog. The vet is about to speak, when Joyce having seen her uncertainty, cuts in.

'I saw your colleague last week. They told me. He told me. Nice young man. It's cancer in her brain, behind her eyeball.'

Finally the vet gets a chance to speak.

'What is the name please? Let me have a chance to look up the records.'

Joyce gives her the details and the vet, looking at the screen, talks to them.

'I see. I see. My colleague said that the tumour was inoperable and that putting Queenie to sleep was the kindest option for her.'

She turns to look at Joyce.

'Yes, that's right.'

'Okay, I understand. Let me just have a look at her.'

The vet moves to look at the dog on the table. She holds Queenie's head and examines the bulge from the tumour. She takes her stethoscope and listens to her heart and breathing.

Steve and Joyce watch as she works. The dog is cowed and submissive.

'I agree her tumour is bad and her heart and breathing are getting more irregular. It does make sense to put her to sleep. Do you want to be here while it happens?'

For the first time, Joyce shows uncertainty. Until now, the vet thought this woman was being a hard-hearted farmer at the end of her working dog's life, but now she can see that is not the case.

'Yes. Yes, Steve and I will stay,' Joyce replies quietly.

The vet is privately disappointed. The moment of death is emotional for many owners, and it's easier for many not to be there. She consoles herself that this woman looks like a tough nut.

'Are you happy to hold her and help me, or shall I get a nurse to help?'

'Is there a difference in cost?'

'It costs a little bit more for a nurse, but many people prefer not to hold their pet, and sometimes they struggle a bit.'

'Steve will hold her,' she asserts, without even glancing at him for his agreement.

The vet prepares the equipment. The drug, the needles, the clippers on the side on the sideboard. She talks to Joyce.

'Now if you could talk to Queenie and Steve if you could stand the other side of the table and hold her close to you. I need to start by shaving a small patch for the needle and then raising a vein.'

Queenie is quiet while all this happens. Joyce strokes her head and talks to her about herding sheep. Steve holds her close. Finally, the vet, head down to the front paw, speaks again.

'I have got the needle in. I am not sure she even noticed. I am ready, if you are ready? Are you ready?'

Joyce has now turned her face down to meet Queenie's upturned head. Queenie licks Joyce's hand, sensing something is wrong. Steve looks on, holding back. Joyce makes the smallest grunt in response, to indicate her agreement. As the anaesthetic slips into her vein, the body relaxes. The vet motions Steve to lay her flat on the table. Joyce follows Queenie's head down. Queenie feebly licks Joyce's hand and then face for the last time.

There is silence as the dog slips away. Nothing in the room moves.

Then from Joyce comes the tears, quickly followed by rasping sobs, as she tries to draw breath between the waves of tears that engulf. Steve too is fighting back the tears. This dog has changed his life too.

'Oh, my love, Queenie. My love. Goodbye. It was just you and me for so long. You were there. You were there. You were there. Just you and me.'

It is for a full minute that the only sound in the room is Joyce's tears and goodbyes. Eventually, she stands up. As she does so she turns to Steve and hugs him, holding onto him for a few seconds.

The vet hasn't known where to look, or what to say throughout all this.

'I am sorry. I can see she was a very special dog.'

She looks at Joyce's tear-stained face. At this point, Joyce takes the vet's hands in both of hers and looks at her young face, strokes her cheek with the back of her hand, and says –

'Thank you. Thank you.'

She then turns to her companion and says in a hollow voice, 'Come on, Steve, let's take her home and bury her high up in the top field above her flock.'

Before the vet can protest, or even react, Steve picks up Queenie's limp body in both arms and carries her across the waiting room, full of waiting animals and owners.

The vet was the brightest in her class. She learnt about all those diseases, all those animals, all those bones and ailments. But what can't be taught is how to respond to owners whose hearts pour out to their dying animals. What can't be taught is how to make the end of life for a precious family friend a beautiful death, a dignified death, a death worthy of their life. How to give a loved pet a beautiful farewell can only come with experience.

24. An awkward question

Tuesday 12th October

'Where do you come from?' Jess asks.

It is an October afternoon. Jess and Ashley are walking, slowly, back to his house after school. She wheels her bike. They are developing their routine. They walk home together. They cross the Portinscale footbridge. They sometimes buy snacks and a drink in a cafe. They share their jokes and use nicknames and have a language all of their own. They have gone from brittle competition to a gentle loving routine. Whereas when couples start out they watch every word to make sure it impresses, now they just babble to each other. They say things and share thoughts that only lovers share.

It is a simple question, or, at least, to her it is. But she has never asked him. She has wondered many times why he looks the way he looks. She wondered the first time she saw him in her class as she saw his tall gangly frame and messy, frizzy hair. He hears a completely different question to the one she is really asking.

Ashley looks at her puzzled, so she asks again, 'Where do you come from?'

'You know where I come from. I come from East London, from Bethnal Green.'

'I know you come from London, angel. But you aren't from London, are you?'

He still looks baffled. She tries again.

'You're not all "British" are you? Some of you is from…another country. Right?' As the words come out, she realises that what she thought was a straightforward question is anything but that to Ashley. She is moving into unknown territory, perhaps prying into something which is very personal.

'My mum, you know you've met her, is from London. And my stepdad was Italian, or half Italian. I never remember. We came here to leave him behind. He was a complete shit.'

They look at each other. She realises she has strayed into a place that she never expected or intended. He has no idea who his dad is. He has no idea why he has such a frizzy mop of hair or skin the colour of cappuccino. Maybe he has never thought about it or maybe he has buried it so deeply to pretend it isn't there.

'Never mind,' she says. 'Have you done your Geography homework? What a stupid question. Course you haven't. I was going to ask to copy it?'

By now the fell-runner's mother and sister are used to Jess visiting after school. They are both big fans. His mother sees her as the girl who has made him wear deodorant and brush his hair and care about dancing. Before she arrived, he wolfed his food at meals, read a magazine and left as quickly as he could. Now Jess likes to stay to chat with them both, so Ashley stays as well. Ashley's sister is also a big fan of Jess. Given the choice, an elder sister would be much better than an older brother, but if your brother brings home a girlfriend you can look up to, then that's nearly as good.

So Jess does diplomacy and chat for both of them. She shows Emily how to do her make-up. She talks about the music that Emily likes and offers to let her borrow clothes for parties. Jess may be on the tom-boy side of girliness, but she can do the girly talk with the best of them.

On that day, they both pretend they never talked about where he came from. But, in both of their heads, they go over the conversation again and again.

She can't believe it is something he has never thought about. Or does he know very well what she is talking about, but he just doesn't want to talk about it with her? How can he not see that he is of mixed race, not English and Italian, but English and African, or something like that? But what if he doesn't know the secret that his mother is hiding?

The thoughts are equally questioning in his head. How could he be so blind? So stupid? He always knew that he wasn't 'white' like his sister. But in London, there was every spectrum of colour at school and nobody ever asked where he was from so he has never given it much thought. In Keswick, his skin colour is much more obvious; in a town of white people he must stick out. He realises that his skin is an issue and he rethinks, re-sees incident after incident since he arrived. He stood out in school not just because he was a new boy but because he was mixed race.

When Jess has left and his sister is upstairs in bed, he and his mother are alone in the kitchen.

'Mum, who is my dad? Jess asked me where I come from. I realised I don't know.'

'Your dad?' she blusters. She hadn't been expecting this question and it takes her by surprise. It shouldn't have done. She has been dreading being asked it for as long as she can remember. But now when it comes, she is unprepared. So she lies. Sadly for her, she had forgotten why it wouldn't wash.

'Your dad? You know who your dad is. He is the reason that we moved up here. You should remember him. He was the one you hit over the head with a saucepan.'

Her weak attempt at humour falls flat.

'Nice try, Mum, but I can remember life before Roberto. He only moved in when I was about ten. So, who was my dad?'

His mum is forced to back track.

'Of course, you are right. I thought you meant your stepdad. Your real father, I am ashamed to say, was a colleague at work. I was young, in my early twenties, and I met him when I was training at my first job at a hospital. He was a doctor and we got flirty and had a few one night stands. I thought I was taking precautions but not enough. Nine months later you came along. I never even told him. I am sorry, I should have told you a long time ago.'

She is lying. He knows she is lying. But he doesn't want to push it, so he lets it go. He will need to find another way, need to wait another day to find out who his father is.

He lies in bed that night, unable to sleep. A day that began so normally has seen him get brittle with Jess, listen to his mother lie to him, and most of all, left him absorbed in thought about who his father is. He has often wondered about what he wants to do with his life. Now he is wondering where he came from, asking himself why he is so sure that his mum is lying, and asking himself why should she lie. It will take another week before he has the answer to those questions.

25. Talking about families

Friday 15th October

It is the Friday after Jess asked 'that question'. Jess is busy so the fell-runner has gone to help the shepherdess on the farm. He doesn't normally go on Fridays, but he wants to talk to someone.

When he arrives, he tells her he was sorry to hear about Queenie. Joyce smiles weakly and tells him that she isn't sure she will get another dog, and the grief of losing a pet is too hard, and the training of a new one too difficult a task.

It is a quiet time of year for sheep farmers. The lambs have mostly gone to market. The rams are out with the ewes. The farm is readying for winter. Joyce and the fell-runner are preparing the sheep shed for the lambing season by mending the hurdles, repairing the shuttering, and putting in new storage bins. They work together; sometimes in silence, sometimes in conversation.

Once the work has finished, they go inside, she for a cup of tea, and he to enjoy a biscuit. Their music sessions have continued, but they have also changed. The awkwardness of the early sessions has gone. They use their time now to discuss what is on their mind. They give each other a kind of mutual therapy. They can talk and the other will listen. It is an unusual friendship. They both tolerate each other's music, but it is the chance to talk that they really relish. He puts his music on first. They have a routine now. The simple question begins their dialogue.

'How was your week?' she asks, sensing that he has come here for a reason.

'My week – my month,' he corrects himself, 'my month has been different. Weird. Jess asked me where I came from. I told her I came from London. She asked where did I really come from, and I didn't know what she meant, but then it became clear that what she really meant was, why wasn't I white? Where did the bit of me that wasn't white come from?'

'Isn't that a pretty straightforward question?'

'It should be. It should have been. You might think I would have been asked that question a few times, but I haven't, or at least I haven't been asked at an age when I knew that what my mum says isn't true. I have never really given my skin colour any thought. It certainly wasn't an issue down south. I had never really thought about it because I was like so many others in London. Up here I stick out like a sore thumb. My mum told me I was the result of a brief fling with a work colleague. I might have believed it normally but I could tell she was lying. I don't know how, but I could just tell. But why would she lie? That's what I don't understand.

'I have gone from knowing who I was and having a sense of identity to not knowing anything about myself. I know nothing about my dad and now I want to. As a result, I now question everything I used to take for granted. My feeling of identity has gone. Something that I never knew I had has gone, and it unsettles me. I don't know how I can get it back.'

They sit in silence as his music plays. When it finishes, she stands up.

'I guess you need to find out who your dad was, or is. Now I am going to play you some Beethoven. Of all the composers he has the power to move me. I listen to this, his 9th symphony, and I feel "wow".'

She laughs as she realises how ridiculous that sounds.

'Why are you here?' he asks. Jess has questioned him and now he decides to question Joyce.

'How do you mean?'

'You know just what I mean. Why are you here? Why are you in this farmhouse with your sheep and your dogs? You've got children but I hardly hear about them. What is your story? It's funny I never thought about anybody's identity till somebody asked me. Now I look around and in my head I ask the same question of everybody. Who are they? Where do they come from? What is their story? And I realise I have no idea what your story is.'

She looks at him. Suddenly she feels like she is being interrogated, and she can't decide whether to confess or keep quiet. There are things she has never spoken of, and least of all to somebody who is young enough to be her grandson. But like the killer who wants to confess, she wants to talk. She may not tell the whole story today but she wants to talk.

'I was a nurse. He was a doctor.'

Ashley realises that this is the same pairing as his mother has lied about.

'We were both young. We were both good looking. It's hard to believe that when you look at me now; old and grey.'

She sighs and continues, 'So we were young and beautiful and we moved in the same circles. We had the same friends. The aim of every nurse was to catch a doctor. The aim of many doctors was to bed a few nurses. However, once we began, bit by bit we became closer. We dated. We got engaged. We got married. That makes it sound so simple, and perhaps it was. My family were delighted that I was dating a doctor. They were very ambitious for me. They were very traditional too. For my conservative parents, the idea that a couple might live together without marriage was unthinkable, so they put pressure on me to marry. So we did. Today, it would never happen. Two people would share a house and discover they weren't suited, but not in those days.

'So we got married. Everybody thought we were the perfect couple. It's true that we looked good together. He brought in the money and I made the perfect home. We had children, three children. And for many people that would have been enough, to have a rich professional husband, gorgeous children and a lovely house. That should have been enough. But little by little, I realised I wasn't happy. I wanted to be loved, really loved.

'When I left him, those who knew him said that he did really love me. They were probably right, but he loved me for what I represented, for what his upbringing told him his life should be. He didn't love me as a person, but as a possession. He loved me the way these dogs love me. Unquestioning. Unswerving. These dogs would love anybody who fed them and walked them and worked them. And he was like that.

'But I wanted to be loved for me, as an individual. I wanted to know he was choosing me. It became an obsession. I needed to know that I was loved for being me, not because I was the demure wife who made his life complete. I tested him, tested our marriage. He scolded me and then forgave everything. So, when the kids came of age, I left him. I left him to find myself and find some of that individual passionate, unique love that I crave. I went overseas for a few months to do some of the things I had never done.

'He never understood. How could he? He loved me the only

way he knew how. It just wasn't the way I wanted to be loved. The children all saw his side of the story. They said he was a broken man. They could see his pain, and they had all grown up with parents who never argued. But even though he was so broken, he soon remarried. The kids had a happy home, so they didn't really understand. It was only when they began to have relationships of their own that they began to have some kind of inkling about why I had done what I did.

'I came here to start my new life. I knew that close to fifty I would find it hard to find new love but I could be my own boss. I used my divorce money to buy this farm and learnt how to farm sheep. Because I have got what I deserved, I am something of a hermit. I never did find the love I craved and I am surrounded by my dogs and my sheep who love me just the way I objected to being loved by my husband. How crazy is that? But the hills, and the seasons and the new challenges give me a satisfaction that I lacked before.'

In her voice and the corner of her eye there is just a trace of a tear. The fell-runner asked for her story and he has been given it. The smallest, simplest thread of a question has been pulled and unravelled to reveal so much more.

26: Humiliation on the fells

Thursday 21st October

Jess's family farm stands high up in the Newlands Valley. Beyond the shepherdess, beyond the beaten track, nestles Maiden Moor Farm. It has a few fields farmed for centuries by Jess's parents and their parents before them, and back through the generations. It is a beautiful farm, an old slate farmhouse, slate barns and five hundred ewes spread over the surrounding hills. Through the middle of the farm runs a quiet beck.

While most children grow up with a bike ride in the park for exercise, Jess grew up herding sheep and running up the fells before breakfast. Before breakfast on a Sunday, she can run up the valley from her farm towards Dale Head, along Hindscarth Edge and Littledale Edge, and stand on Robinson to look down the Newlands Valley and then back down High Snab bank. The route is a round four or five miles, 1,000 feet up and 1,000 feet down.

This is the heritage that Ashley is contending against, and, of course, he is in the men's race, not the women's race. Ashley is racing not against Jess, but against her brothers, Kevin and Jim, on Saturday. Jess and Ashley may both be in the under-eighteens category, but they are racing alongside adults.

Jess has invited Ashley to visit the farm one afternoon after school. She shows him around. They look at the barn where the sheep come in at lambing time. He compares its size and tidiness to Joyce's barn with amazement. He sits on a tractor for the first time and she laughs at him and takes a picture on her phone.

In the corner of the barn is a pen holding a sheepdog bitch and her puppies. Eight small bundles of fur, they clamber at the sides of the pen when they see Jess and Ashley appear.

'They are so cute. How old are they?'

'About six weeks now. They'll be ready to leave their mum in about a month. My dad thinks they are better as adults if they stay a little longer.'

'What do you do with them? Can I have one?'

'Only if you have £1000 to spare, Ash...'

'£1000!' he interrupts. 'You cannot be serious, Jessica! £1000. They give them away in London. You're not serious, are you? You are winding me up.'

'Oh, I am very serious,' she replies, holding his chin playfully in her hand so he looks at her. 'My dad is a big sheepdog breeder. This bitch is one of the best, and the dad is a champion. He paid a lot just to get her mated with one of the top dogs from the South Lakes. This is big income for us. So you might get a kiss for free from me but not a sheepdog. These dogs may go overseas. The States. Europe. You name it, they go there. A good dog can do more than a fleet of quad bikes can and has brains to boot. This bitch once dug a half-dead ewe out of a snowdrift and stood by it, barking, till my dad came over. And,' she adds, 'it's Jess, not Jessica!'

'And mine name's Ashley,' he retorts with a victorious glance. 'Can I cuddle one?'

'Is that all you can say, "can I cuddle one"? You can cuddle the runt of the litter. Slow and strange colours, just like you.'

He shoots her a dirty look.

'Okay, I take back the strange colours. Here you go. Don't drop her!'

Jess bends over into the pen and scoops up the puppy. It is mostly white, with a black and grey-flecked head and a brown tip to its tail. Ashley cuddles the puppy, which roots into his chest and reaches up to lick the underneath of his chin. He giggles, while she looks on and smiles with the content of seeing him enjoying the things she holds so dear.

'She tickles. What a feeling. What a cute bundle of love. Any time you want to lick me like that, just let me know…' He shoots her a cheeky grin.

'Dream on! You can sleep in the cow barn if that's what you like. They'll be happy to lick you. Come on, put her back. You've yet to meet my brothers, and they aren't quite as cute her.'

She takes him to see her bedroom. It is a strange combination of Jess the girl and Jess the tough fell-runner. She has a shelf full of her running trophies. He picks the big ones up one by one and examines them. She asks him what he is looking at. In a moment of honesty, he explains that he never won a trophy or even a medal for anything. They sit on her bed and he tries to kiss her, but she won't let him. It doesn't feel right, she tells him, to his predictable dismay.

At the kitchen table, Jess's mum has laid out food for them all. Dad is off round the farm somewhere, but the two brothers are there. Jess introduces Ashley and they grunt greetings at each other. While the two women and Ashley sit at the table, Kevin and Jim lean against the work surface, keeping their distance in every sense.

While they may seem rough farm boys, they are as protective of their little sister as Ashley is of his. They worry about her getting hurt, but they also know how much Ashley means to Jess. Winding up their little sister is always a good game and when they hear he is a runner too, they feel protective and mischievous.

It is left to Jess's mum to try and make conversation between these sparring combatants.

'Did Jessica show you the puppies?' she asks.

'Oh yes. I got to hold one. They are very cute. I wanted to have one, but Jessica,' he flashes a cheeky look at Jess as he mirrors her mother's use of her name, 'says they are not cheap.'

'Not cheap at all. All but a couple are already sold. Two of them will be trained here and then go to the States. I hear you are running in the Borrowdale half-marathon, Ashley.'

'I am,' he says, but is interrupted by a voice from behind him.

'So you'll be racing against me and Jim,' Kevin states as a challenge. 'How do you think you'll get on?'

The women could see it. The moment the words had left Kevin's lips, they could see the car crash of a conversation about to happen. They could see the testosterone hanging thick in the air.

Ashley could have said a thousand things in response that would have made the conversation go in a different direction, but he doesn't. He smacks Kevin's challenge straight back. Without turning around to look at his questioner, he responds, 'Jess, says she thinks I'm pretty good. Do you think I should be worried, then?'

'As long as you aren't trying to beat us, not worried at all.'

'I won't be *trying* at all to beat you. It'll be too easy for that.'

'Now, boys, behave. Would anybody like a piece of cake?' The matriarch's attempt at mediation is unsuccessful.

'Are you getting cocky just cos you raced our sister? Don't be fooled by the speed of that fat pudding.' Kevin tips his head towards his sister. Before Jess can respond, Ashley starts to reply.

'I'm not fooled…'

The matriarch calls the sparring to an end. 'ENOUGH, all of you! Jessica, was there any homework the two of you were going to do together? If not, then perhaps it's time for Ashley to go.'

This is the end of his first visit to his girlfriend's farm.

As Jess's mother clears up the table and does the dishes she can hear her daughter, her only daughter, scolding her new boyfriend outside the window. She can't hear all the words. But she catches the word 'idiot' then as Ashley tries to defend himself her daughter words are a little stronger. She sighs. This is not how the first meeting is meant to go. She knows that Kevin is partly to blame. Perhaps the next meeting at the race will be better, she hopes. Who is she kidding.

Saturday 23rd October

A few days later, they are all lined up in Seatoller, ready for the start of the race. The brothers are jibing him at his speed. Jess is refusing to talk to any of them. The men's race starts about thirty minutes after the women's.

So, once the pack of the hundred or so women have set off, Ashley is left trying nonchalantly to avoid the brothers in the pack while they edge closer to him, hoping to bait him some more.

The Borrowdale half-marathon takes in some of the most beautiful and challenging scenery in the Lakes. While most marathons and half-marathons are flat or almost on the level, this race is anything but. It heads due south from Seatoller, past Seathwaite Farm, and up the valley, leaving Green Gable and Great Gable on the right behind Seathwaite Fell and Glaramara on the left. As the valley ends at Great End, the route turns left and heads towards the Langdale Pikes. But, as the runners come through the pass and head downhill, they turn left again and follow the Langstrath Beck back down the valley. If the rains have been heavy, then the race is slower and wetter. As the runners head back towards Borrowdale again, they leave High Raise on their right and Stonethwaite on their left.

Unfortunately for Ashley, the hapless fell-runner, the brothers are determined to lure him to humiliation. Their approach is simple; one brother will encourage him to run too fast early on, and then the second brother will take over the lead.

The route of the half-marathon is part-fell race, part road race; half flat, half climb. These brothers are experienced on these slopes, just like their sister.

The route up the road to Seathwaite Farm is easy enough, and the pack of runners set off. The weather is neither kind nor cruel. No beautiful sunshine on an autumn day nor driving rain – just overcast. It's fine weather for a race.

The brothers have agreed that Kevin will lead, as he is better at running uphill, and Jim will deliver the killer blow. Kevin is tall and, like most farmers, he is sandpapered by the weather. His tall frame supports his muscular physique. Most hill farmers are fit from their occupation – the demands of their jobs make them so – but Kevin and Jim are runners too, so they are perfectly tuned.

Ashley takes their bait. As Kevin pulls away, Ashley follows. If Jess were there, she would spot the trap at once and would have told him, but Ashley is on his own and has made a bad mistake.

The race is right in the heart of the Lakes. Out from Seatoller is a long valley and at the far end is a wall of rock. But for the first five or so miles, the runners head up the valley from which there appears to be no escape. This is the view that the Romans saw, that Coleridge and Wordsworth saw, a view that has barely changed in five hundred years. Up this great valley,

Kevin is pulling Ashley forward, luring him gently, step by step, into exhaustion.

By mile five, the pack is spreading out. Jim is biding his time in the centre of the pack. Kevin is third behind two national runners and Ashley is about fifty yards behind in sixth place. Behind them, the other runners are straggled out, beads on a necklace, down the valley.

The wall of rock at the end of the valley appears, from a distance, to have no route out. It does but the climb is hard and steep. And the brothers' plan is to wait till Kevin has wrung Ashley out once the wall is climbed. Jess has let slip that Ashley is better at climbing than coming downhill. And so, as Ashley reaches the top of the valley's end, spitting phlegm and lungs aching, he is still in sixth place and Kevin is still third. But to Ashley's amazement (and delight) he begins to catch up with Kevin after half a mile from the end of the wall. However, his amazement turns to horror as the descent at the far end of this vast horseshoe begins.

The brothers have planned well. Kevin is faster going uphill and Jim is faster downhill. So, as Ashley is catching Kevin, Jim is catching Ashley.

As the descent begins, Ashley overtakes Kevin, but seconds later Jim overtakes Kevin, and they grin as he passes. Thirty seconds later he overtakes Ashley with a sarcastic 'How ya doing, Ash?' as he passes.

As the race continues, there are a hundred minor dramas being played out on this course; runners whose tendons have sprained, young girls who overtake their rivals, slips and slides that bang knees. Ahead of Ashley and the brothers is Jess, steaming to a respectable third place in the women's race.

The drama of this race day is with Ashley, Kevin and Jim and their tussle for supremacy. Jim is in the lead and stepping up the pace on the downhill section. Ashley is trying to keep up. He is pushing his legs harder than he has ever done before.

Jim's lead continues to grow, his pace and rhythm are effortless. Now, as Ashley's legs tire, he begins to slow down.

Jim crosses the line in fourth position. Eight minutes later, Kevin crosses the line in twelfth position. And four minutes after that, Ashley crosses the line. Jess is waiting at the line for them and she is not fooled. By the smirk on her brothers' faces she can tell that Jim and Kevin have been playing games, but she also knows that Ashley may have walked into a defeat that his own arrogance has engineered.

So when he crosses the line, she is there to greet him. She is there as he staggers over the line and collapses on the grass, his legs jellied by the run. Jess knows something has happened but she doesn't know exactly what. She knows the men she loves have fought, and she knows that her brothers have won. She knows that her man is beaten and exhausted. So she greets him, but doesn't hug him. He was foolish, but she doesn't know whether she should choose family over boyfriend or boyfriend over family, so she does neither.

27. Finding the past

Saturday 6th – Sunday 7th November

Two weeks later, on a cold Saturday evening, Ashley joins his mother and sister as they watch the *X Factor* results. This is yet another one of these changes in his behaviour that neither of them can still quite understand, but like nonetheless. After *X Factor* the news comes on. His mother is about to turn over the channel when the sports announcer mentions the New York Marathon. This catches his attention. The newsreader announces, 'Today's New York marathon was run by the Kenyan runner "Mtoto" Achebe in two hours and seven minutes, a time that is just outside the course record. The Commonwealth and Pan-African champion has now added the New York marathon to his achievements.'

'Hey, he looks just like you,' his sister jokes. 'He's tall and skinny with arms and legs that go all over the place. He even shares Mum's nickname for you. That must be because he's a big baby like you.'

'Haven't you got something useless to do, like messenging or texting, or polishing your toe nails?' he jibes back.

'No, I'm waiting for *Xtra Factor*. Can we turn over now, please?'

He obliges. As he turns back from his sister to the screen, he notices his mother sitting staring fixedly at the screen, trying desperately to look disengaged and innocent. In a split second, what is an innocent remark by his sister takes on new importance as he registers the look on her face.

When he eventually does get to bed, his mind goes over and over the incident. Why would his mum look like that about his sister's comments about the winner of the New York marathon? Why?

Then he begins to wonder if there could be a connection between himself and such a great runner. What if his mother reacted so strangely not because she was embarrassed about his nickname, cross about her children bickering, or worried about his running, but because his sister is right? He does look like the runner. He does share a nickname, and there must be a reason. Is that because the athlete is his father, or reminded his mother of his father? What if his father is Kenyan? What if his father is a Kenyan athlete? Maybe his running is part of his identity. He laughs to himself at how a chance remark and his interpretation of a look on his mother's face has made his imagination run riot. But each time he tries to shrug off the ridiculous notion, his mind brings it boomeranging back.

The enormity of the possibility of this wild, mad idea makes it hard to sleep. In his head, he dreams of couples dancing round and round an enormous dance floor, and the winner of the marathon grabbing him and asking him to dance. Ashley realises he is dressed for this, while the runner is in his athletic gear. They then set off round the floor, tangoing at twice the speed of the other couples. In this dream, he and the marathon runner are the same size and the same shape, and mirror each other's movements. They dance together wonderfully, beautifully, but in doing so, the other dancers are pushed out of the way.

He realises that he cannot answer his own questions. He needs to know his mother's secret but, before he confronts her, he decides to see if he can find any evidence in their house.

He hides in his room, pleading homework, till his mother and sister go out at lunchtime. There are two places that his mother might hide emotional baggage: in her bureau in the hall, or in her bedroom. He tries the bureau in the hall first, but he finds only bills and bank statements, so he goes to her bedroom. He has no qualms about searching the bureau but her bedroom makes him a lot more uneasy. He starts under the bed where he finds nothing except old clothes that she never wears. He tries her chest of drawers, his ears twitching in case they return early. He finds nothing but the lingerie legacies of relationships that are no longer.

He looks around. The wardrobe is the next best place. Lots of shoe boxes. He opens the first couple of boxes, but they just have shoes in them, which he supposes shouldn't be a surprise. He tries the top cupboards but finds only old unwanted clothes, waiting for Oxfam to claim them. He sits on the bed, defeated. If they aren't here, then the only other place they could be is the loft.

He stares around him, working out where else his mother might keep her emotional past. He looks again. He tries her bedside cabinet drawers. Nothing. He tries one last thing he saw in a movie, where the vital photograph was taped to the underneath of a drawer. He doesn't believe for a moment his mother would do something like this but he tries. He finds nothing taped to the drawers in her dresser, but there is one drawer left in the bedside cabinet.

And there it is. Something taped underneath her bedside cabinet drawer – hidden from the greasy Italian perhaps. He holds the drawer up. It's an unsealed envelope. The glue has yellowed and hardened with age. He waits for a moment. This could be what he has been looking for, or it could be nothing. He breathes in and holds his breath for a second and then pulls the content from the envelope.

Inside it he finds a photograph, two letters and a couple of postcards. The photograph taken many years ago is of his mother and a tall black man, perhaps an African he guesses. He looks at the postcards and they have Kenyan stamps.

The letters are in a simple almost childlike hand. He looks again at the photograph which could have been taken in Kenya. Maybe he was right after all. His mum is much younger, and she looks very happy with a broad smile. She has her arms around a man. He is tall and wiry and smiling too. They are both dressed in shorts and a T-shirt. It is a picture of a couple enjoying each other. In another setting, it could be an ordinary holiday snap. But he knows this is important; it's the roots of his life. Is this a photo of his father?

He turns to the letter and postcard. The date is a few months before he is born. The first is a standard holiday blurb. 'Lovely to meet you. Special time. Come back soon,' and so on. The second stops him; this is what he has been looking for. His heart races. The card says simply, 'A baby. Our baby. Come back, and we can marry and live together. He will be our little "Mtoto". Love, Isaiah.'

His father is Kenyan. His nickname is the one his father gave him. His sister was right. He doesn't know whether to laugh or cry, to smile or weep. The pieces of his life are beginning to re-order and make sense again. He puts the bundle down on the bed. He needs to ask his mother so many questions. He replaces all the objects in the envelope and puts the drawer back in its original position.

Later, when his mother and sister return home, he retreats

to his room. He is bursting to ask her questions and he knows that his face will betray him if he sees her now. His mum shouts up the stairs and ask if he wants a drink. He declines. He is monosyllabic in his behaviour for the rest of the day. He wants the whole conversation with her. At tea, he reads a magazine and acts like they aren't there. Eventually, his sister goes to bed and he has his mother to himself. He has now realised that this is not an easy conversation for him to start, or for her to finish. So, he starts from where they last left off. She is watching telly.

'Mum, who was my dad?'

She tries the same lie again. 'I told you the other day that he was a work colleague.'

'No, Mum, he wasn't. Tell me about Kenya.'

Up until this point she has tried to stay watching telly, pretending to give him only half her attention. At the word 'Kenya', she stops and looks at him. He wonders if this is what the face of a murder victim looks like just before death. He has her complete attention. Her face is frozen, her pupils dilated, and she knows the game is up.

'Kenya?' she repeats, stalling for time.

'Yes, Kenya. Isn't that where you met my dad?' he bluffs.

She could have replied with many things that would have told him that he was mistaken. In fact, it isn't words that give her answer, but her face and her body language slowly change. Her realisation that a great secret she has carried with her for so many years will now be lifted. He watches her body relax and mould into the sofa and feels that he can see her tension ebb away. She wants to talk – after all these years, she wants to talk.

'I am sorry. I should have told you years ago. There was never a right moment, and the longer I kept the secret, the harder it became to tell you.'

She starts again.

'Kenya is where I met your dad. I wasn't there for long. Just went for a week or two's holiday with some girlfriends. We stayed in a beach resort up the coast from Mombasa.'

She pauses. He sees her changing as she tells the story. He sees her almost return to the carefree woman of a different life. Her eyes are moist even as every word is being forced out.

'He was the sports coach. He carried himself differently from the other Africans at the resort. It sounds corny, but he stood tall and proud. All the women noticed him almost straightaway. He had a charisma about him. In those days, I was much better looking than I am now.

'On the second day, I played a game of tennis with him and afterwards we had a drink at the bar. He was relaxed and friendly. Conversation was easy. He was clever and funny. He was trying to earn a living as a coach and become a professional runner.'

She stops and she looks directly at her son. 'So, when I see you running, when I see how good you are, when I see you are your father's son, I am so proud. I know he would be so proud. I was amazed when you disappeared when we first arrived and it turned out you were running.'

She stops, choked with emotion. There are too many things to say all at once. Her emotional reserve is gone. She returns to her story.

'We talked. We swam in the sea. We spent all our time together when he wasn't working. By the end of the week we cried when we parted. We promised all sorts of things about how we would keep in touch. But, of course, we weren't equals. No matter how hard I tried, he was just a holiday romance. I think I knew that all along…but it was a wonderful few days.

'And then back home, a few weeks later, I discovered I was

pregnant. I thought I had taken precautions. I didn't know what to do. He rang me. I had given him my address and telephone number. I didn't think he would use it. So when I didn't return his letters he called. I told him more out of desperation than anything, and then he said we should marry. I felt so guilty. I never talked to him again after that. I sent him a letter telling him that I had lost the baby, but I knew I wanted to keep it, wanted to keep you, and I am so glad I did.

'Telling you…it has been this big secret…I have never known how to tell you, when to tell you, what to tell you. And as the song says, "a secret like a cancer grows". I should have told you the other day when you asked. There are a thousand times I should have told you.' She pauses to see her son's reaction.

The son has been watching the mother. He has seen her change as she talks. He can see the emotion that is tied up in her, the burden that is being lifted from her shoulders.

'What was his, my dad's, name?'

'Isaiah Ombati. Isaiah. Isaiah,' she repeats, rolling the name round her mouth like a long-forgotten taste.

'Where is he now?'

'I have no idea. I have no idea whether he made it running. I shut him out of my mind. The guilt about the way I treated him kept him out. How did you know about Kenya?'

It is his turn to lie.

'I guessed. When Emily spotted the likeness and the nickname in the New York marathon, it was like a light bulb. That runner was Kenyan, so I wondered if my father had been Kenyan. You know how I have been thinking about these things. A month ago, Emily's comment would probably have gone straight over my head, but yesterday they made sense. And your face when Emily teased me, trying so hard to look innocent, really meant you weren't. So I lay awake last night thinking about it. I googled the nickname and discovered it meant baby or little one. And after that, I guessed.'

They are both awkward now. She has told him her big secret. He has discovered more about his roots in ten minutes than he has known before in all his life. His mum breaks the silence.

'I am really sorry that it has taken you this long to find out. It's funny, isn't it? I thought that moving to the Lakes might bring about many changes in our lives, but I never guessed it would be the reason that I told you all about your father.'

He is not going to give her forgiveness now – or a hug.

'Mum, it's a lot better having a dad who is a Kenyan runner than a violent wife-beater from the East End.'

She smiles weakly, as if there are more things to be said.

He goes to bed. As he lies in bed wide awake, something Jess said when they first raced up Wandope comes hurtling back into his brain. He has to tell her what he knows. He has to tell her, because his search for his identity has come between them. He can see the pair of them at the end of their run on Wandope, early on that Sunday morning, the last trace of morning chill fading, and the sun rising high. He sees them after the race on Wandope, that first beautiful encounter finished, when he was on his knees, desperate for breath.

He remembers Jess saying, 'If you haven't been training for years, it's like you were born to run.'

Now he knows that he was.

28: Swopping secrets

Saturday 13th November

There are people who keep their secrets for years, and there are people who want to know secrets for much of their lives. A secret between two people is a splinter in the flesh of a relationship. It stops things ever quite being right, from ever being quite being whole, as the fell-runner and his mother have just discovered.

So it is for the prisoner and the estate agent, for Steve and for Hazel. They have walked and they have sex. Their desire is blooming while their love is withering, because they both cannot be sure what the revelation of their secret will bring. They are frozen in the fear of not knowing if the truth will be worse than the lies.

And, one cold sultry November afternoon as the low winter sun dimly lights the fells, she can take no more. Hazel wants to be in love, wants to feel there are no secrets. She wants to know that he loves her despite her illness. She wants to know who or what is the secret that is not the wife.

She picks him up at the farm in her car. She has planned all this. She drives him up the short distance to the pass between the Newlands Valley and the Buttermere Valley. She parks where they can see the whole way down the valley. She has said nothing of her plans. They have made small talk since he got in. The dogs are going frantic in the back. He looks at her, feigning puzzlement, but he senses what is about to come. He knows without words.

She starts to speak. She has turned off the engine. She reaches out her hand to hold his but she looks the other way. She does not want him to see her eyes or her tears or her fear.

'I can't go on not knowing,' she says, still looking out of the window. His stomach turns over. Her first tear escapes. 'I have to know why. I have to know why you can only meet me on Saturdays and why you pretend to live on the farm, and if it isn't a wife, who or what is it that you are hiding from me.'

She pauses. 'And I have to tell you. I have to tell you my secret.' These last words she squeezes out.

'Your secret?' he stutters. It never occurred to him that she might have a secret.

'Oh God, Steve, I am so scared. I am so scared that whatever you tell me will put an end to us, or what I am about to tell you will put an end to us.'

He squeezes her hand. He is embarrassed. He is close to tears. 'You go first.'

'I have Parkinson's Disease,' she says simply.

They look at each other, not sure how to cope with each other's information. Neither was expecting this. Neither was prepared, and their defences, prepared for all sorts of battles, are useless. She begins to laugh nervously. He laughs unconvincingly too. For a moment the clouds lift and they are dancing. They are in each other's arms. They are twirling across the dance floor but it is a dance to which neither of them knows the steps. They must hold each other tightly and learn. The dance is hard and long but they are young and have years to learn the steps. The clouds come down again. The pain is not over yet.

He too had thought of all the reasons why this beautiful, adorable woman would be free to meet with him, and he never thought of a disease.

'I have so many questions. Tell me everything and I will tell you everything.' Her secret is said. She has passed the first hurdle. There is a lot more she still wants to say.

His hand reaches out to hers again and he pulls her hand up to his face. She continues, 'We can't stop now. We can't leave this car till we are done.'

Hazel turns her face away again and starts talking again. Her breath condenses on the window as she talks.

'I was several years out of university. I had saved some money. I was making plans for the things I wanted to do. I went on holiday to Greece with some friends. It was an idyllic. We lay in the sun, we swam, we sailed and we went clubbing. In the last week we went sailing. While we were sailing my finger got bashed. The finger was bruised, but it didn't bleed; instead, it twitched. A week later it would still twitch. I'd wake in the morning and it might as well have been operated by some manic remote control.

'A month later it was still not right. I went to my GP and they said it would get better and told me to come back. And then I noticed the side of my foot was numb. More doctors. More investigations. They ruled things out They asked about my life in minute detail. They told me it was a spinal problem, and then they ruled that out after an MRI scan. They told me it was just stress and then they ruled that out.

'After three years I went to see a neurology consultant. I sat in his tiny office and he told me he thought that I had Parkinson's Disease. He was cold and clinical. He gave me a leaflet. "Any questions, just ask," he said, but I felt he was in a hurry so I left in a daze.'

She takes a deep breath. Her eyes were still looking through the wet glass and on to the hilltop. She pauses and continues, 'I could tell you every last detail of every symptom I have had. It doesn't make for easy listening and it's not going to make you love me any more.'

She shoots him a glance. He is staring at her. He makes no expression. His face is taut with listening; even the dogs are quiet.

'Tell me the symptoms. I need to understand.'

'The younger doctors were amazing, but I should have been flirting with them. They were young and eligible and the women could have been my friends. I remember thinking that. These people had become my carers when they should be my companions.

'My symptoms? I will tell you my symptoms. My muscles stop working properly. They become like a record with a scratch. I stop, then start. I am like a computer which crashed. My brain wants me to move. But my body doesn't respond. And then when I move I can't stop. That's why I walk the hills. Exercise is good for me. Sex is good for me. Dancing is good for me. Once I start moving, I can keep going. But my facial expressions are starting to go. My hand is getting out of control. That's why I hold the lead in my left hand. It stops it being lifeless by my side.

'I have become the master of disguising my symptoms, but perhaps I cannot hide everything. You've commented. That second walk in Grange, when you told me not to run off, and I said it was Rose and you looked at me strangely. You were right; it wasn't Rose. It was Parkinson's.

'I am now on medication many days. If I wasn't, my smile would be gone. My hand would be lifeless except for a tremor.

If it were a bad day, I might be frozen to my chair. I have taught Rose to lick my face when I am frozen and that helps unlock me. But if I take too much medicine I become like a writhing snake; always moving. My muscles go from frozen to perpetual motion.

'So I took the decision to move up here. Where every year when I could walk was a blessing. I wanted to do the things I had thought I might do when I retire. We came here as children on holiday.

'So now I live my life on a tightrope. I have to be careful what I eat. Exercise helps so I walk. Illness makes my symptoms worse, so I have to be careful not to get ill. Five years after my diagnosis, I never imagined that I could find love. Parkinson's makes me feel that I am unlovable. Rose keeps me sane. She doesn't care I have Parkinson's. She loves me, loves the hills…'

Her voice trails off. And then with a final heave she adds, 'And then back in March, out walking, I meet you. And only the other day I realised that what made you so perfect was that you were hiding something. I didn't know what your secret was. But if the secret was a wife, it meant I could be rejected in love for something that wasn't to do with my disease. To begin with the secret was my friend. In my twisted head that sounded good to me. But now the secret is my enemy.

'Your turn,' she said, 'no questions. Let's get this done. Tell me in a sentence. Tell me, please.'

Silence.

She looks at him, looks into his eyes and mouths the word 'Please.'

'Well,' he says, 'I…I…I am a prisoner.'

She looks at him with bewilderment, without understanding.

'I am a prisoner too. We are all prisoners. I am held hostage by my mortgage. Please tell me…'

He interrupts her and tries again. 'I am a prisoner. I am in prison. Twelve years ago, I murdered someone.' He turns away and doesn't dare look at her till he has forced those words out.

Hazel doesn't know how to react. She has thought of so many reasons why this man might behave as he does. But none of them came close to the truth. In any other situation, they would have laughed at the terrible joke, but not on a brooding November afternoon with the storm clouds about to break.

He gulps and begins.

He needs to decide what to tell her and what not to tell her. He wasn't expecting this conversation today.

'I killed two members of my family.'

He pauses, not sure whether to wait for a reaction or not.

'I lost my temper and in a rage I killed my...'

'No! No...no, no. You're a murderer!'

He pauses when she screams out, and then he looks over at her. At that moment, she pushes open the car door, leans out and is sick on the gravel. She leaves the door open while taking deep breaths. He doesn't know what to say. So he goes on as if nothing had happened.

'The prosecution wanted me to be done for murder. My lawyer said he could get me manslaughter. But I pleaded guilty to murder. I was sentenced to a minimum of twelve years. I was nineteen. And that *was* over eleven years ago. I spent a year waiting for my trial. I am now in the open prison over near Lorton. Back in February, I started doing day release with Joyce on a Saturday. We do jobs around the farm in the morning, and then after lunch, she sends me off to walk the dog.

'And then on a walk I met you. And my life changed. In prison, you get fixed on little things, on mealtimes, on TV programmes, but meeting you has changed my life. I have found what could be love again.'

'Love? Shut up! Shut up! Shut up! You're a murderer,' she cries, but her voice is almost lost among her sobs.

The silence continues. It maybe only lasts thirty seconds, but to each of them it seems an eternity. The order of the telling of their story has suddenly become crucial. She has gone from worrying how anybody could ever love a woman with her illness, to realising that this man killed, murdered, a member of his family in anger.

His story has stopped her Parkinson's being the villain of the piece. Can she love a man who has murdered? She realises with disgust that he has been inside her. She doesn't know what to feel, how to feel. She feels dirty. Violated. Sick. Disgusted.

He had hoped for understanding. If this woman, who has got so close to him without knowing what he has done, cannot see past the deed to the person, what hope does he have? He has so much more he wants to say. He starts to speak but thinks better of it.

For weeks, months, they have both wanted to tell their stories. Their secrets have eaten away inside them. Neither has wanted to keep their dark truths from each other, any longer. But now they are told, it is clear why they are secrets. And now each has told their story, the truth will gnaw, will eat away at their emotions, no less than the secret did.

'Oh my god. Oh my god,' she repeats, over and over again.

They drive back in silence. The dogs never get walked that day. Just when they needed to cement, to reaffirm, to heal their relationship, they have left it as an open wound.

29: Floods!

Wednesday 24th November

It has been raining for two days now. In summer, the rain soaks into the dry earth, filling up the empty lakes and tarns. But by November, everything is full. The lakes are brimming. The soil is soaked. The streams are fit to burst. When the wet, warm air falls as rain over the Lakeland Fells, it soon becomes a torrent, then a flood, and then the flood becomes a disaster.

The rivers and the lakes and the tarns and the ghylls are overflowing. Down in Fitz Park the river Greta, the river that in summer tinkles over the rocks, is now lapping at the banks. The football pitch will soon be under water. The raging waters will strip away tarmac and leave rocks in their places. The raging waters will force their way into front rooms like a gang of violent thugs. They will violate a lifetime of treasured possessions and leave nothing but mud and memories. Dogs and babies, cats and children, grown-ups and grannies are all forced from their houses: evicted, expunged by the rising flood.

What appears on the news are the shops and the homes in the towns where the gorged rivers burst their banks and sweep away bridges and flood homes. These are some of the worst rains that anybody can remember. It has rained for twenty-four hours without stopping. The weathermen are warning. The rescue services are preparing. The sand bags are being filled. And, across the Lakes, everyone is watching the sky, the streams, and the news.

In the farms that cloak the hillsides of the fells, the farms that have been etched out of the thin soil over the centuries, the rains have a different effect. Not for them the stagnant water up to waist level. For them it is the flash floods they fear, caused by the torrents of water that come racing down every beck and ghyll. They fear their sheep will be swept away by the sheer force of water, or that a blocked stream will overflow and in attempting to find a new way down the hillside, will flow straight through the farmhouse or the barns or even sweep away the bridge that is the only link to the outside world.

Jess's family farm is high up in the Newlands Valley. When the rains come, they funnel their way down the valley, and when they are heavy, the water rises and bursts over. When the rain is torrential the farm, the fields, the sheep and the people are at risk of the flash floods that follow. And so it is on this November day. Jess has joined her parents and her brothers in the rain to gather in the sheep and to remove everything they can from the sucking writhing stream of water that they know will hit them. Sheep must be shifted. Everything of value moved to higher ground. They take no chances. They must clear the downstairs of the house. They must move farm machinery and save all that they can.

All the children have been sent home from the schools early before the floods hit. Once home, Jess rings the fell-runner. She tells him that the rains will hit her farm in about four hours. She asks him to come and help. And come he does. In the darkness of the wind and rain he cycles up the valley, secretly pleased that he, despite being a city boy, is seen as useful. However, he is also secretly terrified that he may not be up to the job, that he may not be much use.

Halfway up the valley he comes across a stream, now more like a flood. It covers the road, a torrent of water that making the road impassable on a bike. He has cycled this route a dozen times and never noticed a stream – let alone one that could block the road. He abandons his bike and chains it to a tree, a precaution against flood, not theft.

Before he left home his mother asked if he should wear his wellingtons. It was a sensible suggestion but he rejects it. He opted instead for his running shoes.

Once his bike is chained to the tree, he removes his shoes and wades across the flood. As he does so, he is surprised by the strength of the force of water. It is now dark and he has only the light of his bike torch to guide him.

On the far side he puts his running shoes back on. He then sets off, running to Jess's farm a mile or so up the valley. The road has become a river in places with the escaping water using whatever route it can find. He leaps over the leaves and branches scattered on the ground with the dim light of the torch barely lighting his way. His feet are soaked after a few hundred yards and he wonders whether he made the right choice about his boots.

After ten minutes of running, he reaches the turning for Maiden Moor Farm. Above the wind, above the rain, he can hear a noise. He cannot place the noise and it is probably just as well. It is the stream. It is the sound of water, vast amounts of waters, surging down the valley.

Soon in the distance he can see the lights of the farm. He suddenly realises that he will meet her brothers again, those brothers who beat him in the Borrowdale race. He has not forgotten how they treated him and made it clear that they didn't like a cocky city boy dating their sister. The brothers who humiliated him in their winning of the race. And he suddenly realises how difficult asking him must have been for Jess. How much they must fear the floods.

From his previous visit in daylight, he remembers how the road hugs the left-hand side of the valley and how the farmhouse and the barns are on this side of the valley.

Down the centre of the valley, and of the farm, runs a beck, with three bridges over it. The top and middle bridges are humpback, built years ago from local slate. The downstream bridge is made from concrete. It is this one that tractors go over and that lies much flatter and closer to the river. Between the top bridge and the bottom bridge, it is maybe 600 yards.

On this side of the stream, next to the barns, are the pens where the sheep are sorted and sheared. An old hedge hugs the stream next to the pens and then on the other side of the stream are the fields where the ewes with young lambs are put, where the rams run with the ewes and where in winter the ewes from the lowland breeds are kept.

He walks to the farmhouse and knocks on the front door. He gets no response. He knocks again. He knows they must be here. He texts Jess, *I am here.*

He delicately feels his way round to the far side of the house. He peers through the kitchen window. He goes in through the back door. He greets them quietly, not seeing Jess. For a few moments he stands awkwardly as nobody responds. This family sure know how to make a man welcome. At that moment he see Jess's legs appear down the stairs. He smiles as he sees her. When she spots him, she smiles too and crosses the floor and throws her arms around him and greets him with a loud, 'Ash!'

'Come, we must get all that we can upstairs. Kevin, Jim, and

Dad are outside trying to stop the small ghyll that comes down behind the house from bursting. The flood before last burst in through the utility room and swamped half the downstairs. Everything that we can carry is going upstairs.

He responds with movement and a quiet, subdued, 'Okay.' This is beyond his experience, but for her it appears almost normal.

Her mother appears. 'Hello, Ashley. Thanks for coming. How was the road up?' she asks, but doesn't wait for an answer. 'Let's get these books upstairs.'

They have no boxes left, so they each take armfuls of books and magazines upstairs. Jess's mother then motions them to take the chairs and then the contents of the kitchen cupboards and the CDs and DVDs.

They have just a few hours to decide: what is saved first? Which possessions? What could be left behind?

It is now 9 p.m.

As they continue clearing, Kevin bursts in. He stands dripping in his oilskins by the door. He barely acknowledges Ashley's presence in the room; just a disdainful flick of his eyes and the barest nod of his head even to indicate he had even seen his fellow fell-runner.

'We've done the back ghyll. Unless it's really bad, the house should be safe. But the sheep in the far paddock need bringing in. It looks likely that the main stream is going to burst its banks and flood that field. We can bring them in over the top bridge. I'll need both of you.' He gestures at the two teenagers. 'Jess, get the head torches. Ma, you'd better stay in the house.'

There is no head torch for the fell-runner; instead, he uses his mother's old torch with its fading batteries. He puts his waterproof back on and Jess dons hers. She gives him the most fleeting squeeze of the hand as they leave the house and go out into the wind and the rain. The weather shows no sign of improving. The ground is soaking. Streams have appeared from nowhere and run across the yard.

They can see two bobbing torchlights up the valley, where Jess's brother and father are trying to keep the raging torrent free from obstructions. One blockage can force the water to leave the streambed in minutes. And once freed, once liberated from the stream, the foaming, surging water searches for a place to go. It takes no prisoners. It does not stand still. The free surging, swirling water is what every flooded farmer fears.

All three cross the top slate humpback bridge, nearest the house and at the top end of the yard. Already, the water is reaching the bank of the stream and pushing against the side of the bridge and it won't be long before the space in the arch underneath the bridge disappears altogether. As Ashley walks across, he points the torch into the racing brown debris-filled water, and shudders.

As they move into the field, the first few yards are flooded with the overflow from the stream.

'Come on,' Jess's brother yells above the storm. 'This field will be flooded soon. We need to get the sheep out of here. Jess and you go left, and I will go this way.'

It is too dark for the sheepdogs so the three of them must be human sheepdogs. The fell-runner watches the head torch disappear into the field and he goes the other way. Jess is near him, but he cannot see her face, just her silhouette and the light of her head torch against the floodlights of the yard, now over 100 yards away.

The white of the sheep shows up in their dim torch beams even on a night like this. About fifty of them are huddled together in the far comer of the field. They are the shearlings. This year's lambs that are nearly ready for going to market. They are the income for Christmas. Not needed for breeding, but for meat. If they stay in this field they may get stuck in the mud, be swept away, or even drowned if the full force of the river catches them.

The bobbing torches move closer, and the sheep can see that they are being moved. They begin to shift, to murmur, to stutter as they move closer. Jess's brother moves round in a wide loop to join the others so that the trio can push the sheep along the edge of the field, along the line of the fence. That way the sheep are less likely to split up or panic.

The wind and rain have not let up. The lights of the farm are their beacon and slowly they push the sheep towards the bridge. On a summer's day, with the help of two sheepdogs, Kevin could move them in two or three minutes, and would barely need to move from the centre of the field as the dogs darted back and forth, snapping at the heels of the flock. Any foolish ewe that tried to break ranks would be chased and outrun by the dogs with only the slightest command from the shepherd. But not tonight.

They move the frightened flock towards the bridge. As the sheep hit the flooding, they move slowly, and both Jess and her brother can see that the sheep are wary. They know that some may try and break ranks. The three of them move forward arms outstretched, hollering, shouting, stamping, and willing the sheep to cross the bridge into the relative safety of the yard. The first sheep edge across and then, as if they believe that a troll is under the bridge, as they reach the crest they launch across at top speed. They will not be victims. Soon only ten or so are left. But the last sheep are usually the most truculent, the ones most used to hearing the curses of the shepherd as they fail to follow their peers.

Sure enough, one awkward shearling turns back, and then three more break to go back towards the field. Above the noise of the storm, the brother yells at the fell-runner and points at the farm.

'Keep the others on the far side.'

Ashley understands what he must do, and crosses the bridge to keep the first forty in the yard. Jess and Kevin, trained from birth to work with sheep, move back to redirect the escaped ewes. They have not got far, as Jess has already moved with them to head them off.

A minute later the fell-runner can see the head torches reappearing. Soon he can see the first of the escapees on the crest of the bridge, but as the sheep catch sight of him, they pause. Ashley moves back away from the bridge. The brother pushes up behind them. One last heave and they will be in the yard. He watches as Kevin stands, arm outstretched, yelling on the bridge. Later, he will remember him orange in the glow of the yard light. He will remember the colours, just black and orange, and the driving rain. In the flashbulb of his memory, he will see the expression on the brother's face.

For one second the brother is there, high on the hump of the bridge – and then he is gone. Initially the fell-runner thinks he has crouched or gone back, but then he sees two sheep fall backwards.

The bridge has gone. Weakened by the flood, the stone bridge that has stood for over two hundred years has been washed away. The bridge has gone.

And Jess's brother, Kevin, has been swept away with it.

He hears Jess's scream stuck on the far side, her piercing scream, her terrified scream as she calls her brother's name.

To begin with, he is frozen. When he remembers the moment later, he feels he hesitated for too long, but in fact it is only a second or two.

He can see the head torch in the flood water. There is a chance if he acts quickly. He looks down the yard. In front of him he sees sheep and rain, fences and concrete. He starts to run down the yard, following the raging water. The sheep separate in front of him, but there are several pens between him the middle bridge of the three bridges.

He takes the first pen at speed and tries to vault it but his left leg just catches the top rail and he flips over and he hits the ground on the far side. His torch goes flying. He can feel where his leg caught the rail and a pain shoots up his leg but he grabs the torch and runs on. He glances over at the stream. He can't see the head torch light any more. He is trying to remember which bridge is which. Is the middle one the concrete one or the stone one?

The next pen he also takes at speed. But this time he stiffens his body and his body flies up as his hand goes down to take the impact of this corkscrew motion. He screams in pain as his battered left leg lands. Jess tried to get him to vault gates like this but he wouldn't. In the middle pen is the second bridge. He points the torch towards it but it is as flooded as the first and the water is pushing over it. He decides that his only hope is the bottom bridge.

What will he do at the bottom bridge? How can he save him? Where is Jess? Can her brother swim? What if Kevin can't get under the middle bridge? Is he already dead?

He leaps two more pens. In normal times, his vaults would be beautiful to watch: the arc of his legs reaches up and then he lands perfectly, but here, in this muddy field, there is no one to see and with each landing his leg hurts. On the final vault, he slips in the mud and sheep shit on the far side, and falls headlong. He keeps hold of the torch this time but he is covered in dirt. Filthy.

The bridge is only yards away. He may have run for nothing, or for everything.

At the other end of the yard, still on the other side of the stream, still in the flooded field, Jess is screaming. She too has tried to run the length of the field to catch up with her brother, but their boots and the water and the mud in the field have made this impossible. She is moving as quickly as she can, but she knows that her brother is moving at twice her speed in the flood. She can see Ashley's torch on the far bank. She catches its light in occasional glimpses. She sees it race along the pens. She knows this is Ashley racing to rescue Kevin. She sees the light pause just momentarily by the rails for each pen and a feeling of helpless desperation sweeps over her.

For she knows what the fell-runner does not know; she knows that just below the concrete bridge is a wire fence topped with barbed wire, which stretches across the stream marking the boundary of their land. And below that...below that are the Lower Scab Falls where the stream drops thirty feet almost vertically. If her brother passes the lower falls...

At the concrete bridge, the fell-runner hangs over the side rails of the bridge pointing his torch into the rushing water. The water is flowing over the bridge. He is soaked through. It does not even occur to him that this bridge might go too. He peers into the dark, into the water full of mud and leaves and bracken and branches. He peers into the dark to look for the man who beat him with such relish in the fell race. What does a grown man look like in a raging torrent of water?

His torch then catches a glimpse of yellow of the oilskin. Thirty feet upstream is a patch of yellow like a towel in the water. No head torch, no waving arms, no outstretched hand. This is Jess's brother face down in the tumultuous water. Every time in the years to come when he remembers this night he still cannot put into words what he felt.

The yellow mass races towards him. With one arm he grabs the upright rail of the bridge and with the other he reaches out into the water and grabs Kevin's arm. The arm slips into Kevin's hand as the body is pulled by the water. He holds the brother's hand and feels nothing. No response. Nothing. And the water pulls the hand slowly out of his grasp and the body shoots under the bridge.

'No, no, no, no,' is all he remembers shouting. He has not got this far, this close, for nothing. He springs to the other side of the bridge and grabs the upright rail on the other side. He knows that he cannot hold the body in the raging water by the limp hand so, as the torch spots the body reappearing, he grabs harder. He reaches for the arm and holds it. But he needs two hands or he will not fight the water. For a few seconds he pauses, and then he risks his life to save another. He lets go with his hand from the upright and for a few seconds has no grip, just the weight of his body on the bridge.

Keeping his grip on Kevin's arm with both hands, he swings his legs round so he straddles the metal, upright, with a leg either side. With one hand, he moves his grip and grabs the collar of the jacket and lifts the head out of the water. He then slowly moves his hands round to grab the body under the arm. But with each move, he has to let go a fraction. He can see almost nothing, as the torch was lost when he grabbed the body for the second time. There is just a faint glow from the farm yard lights, 100 yards away.

He now has the brother's head out of the raging water.

However, he is stuck. He has a leg either side of the upright rail. The water is flowing over the top of the bridge. He is holding the body tightly but he cannot get it all the way out of the water without changing his grip. And if he changes his grip, he risks Kevin slipping back into the flood. To begin with, he thinks he will wait for help, but then he fears there will be no help. He doesn't know whether Jess is coming for him or has gone to fetch Jim and her father.

So he decides he has to get the body out of the water. He cannot wait there forever. Still the rain pours down, shaken from the skies, in sheets. He is in the pitch black, bar the faint light from the farmyard, now partly hidden by the trees along the river.

He decides to try and pull out the body by tugging him backwards onto the bridge. He pulls his right leg as far it will go. His buttocks have felt a low concrete ledge where the edge of the bridge is slightly higher than the rest. He needs to use this ledge to push against with his feet. But, no matter how high he lifts his leg, his foot cannot reach the ledge. He risks his grip on Kevin by leaning left so his right leg can push against the ledge further along the bridge and away from his body. This works. The heel of his foot makes contact with the ledge and he heaves with all his might. He and Kevin's limp form are pushed back, back against the flow of the water. He hears Kevin's head hit the side bar of the bridge as he pushes back. But now his left leg is freed too and he wedges his left foot against the narrow concrete ledge. And, with all the force he has left, he pushes back with both feet.

He screams with pain as his left ankle takes the strain, bruised and battered as it already is from his vault over the pen.

But he has succeeded. Both he and Kevin are on the bridge. The water is still flowing over the top of the bridge and is still swirling over them. He turns over on all fours still holding him with one hand. He tries to stand and his ankle gives way. But he still has to get Kevin out of the flood water, whether he is dead or alive. It seems to him that he has struggled for hours, when, in fact, it is only just more than five minutes since he grabbed the body.

He then hears the sweet sound of Jess's call. She has gone to get help, crossing the middle bridge, unaware of the drama taking place on the concrete bridge. She is now coming back down the yard and she hears his scream as his ankle gives way. When she finds them on the bridge, her voice just keeps a lid on her panic.

'Ash, Kevin, oh my God, oh my God, oh my God. Dad! Jim! They're here. They're here!'

'He's not breathing. He's not breathing,' is all that Ashley can manage, and torn between lover and brother, Jess doesn't know what to do.

'We need to empty his lungs. We need to get him breathing. We need to drag him out of the water and towards the farm. Grab that arm.'

Between them, they drag Kevin's form up the track and towards the barns. With every step, his ankle shoots with pain. Clear of the water, Ashley turns Kevin face down and head towards the water. While Jess is still too panicked to think, the cold of the water and the pain from his left leg is keeping him focused. He instructs her to hold the torch on her brother. He then sits astride her brother and begins to pummel rhythmically on his back. His two hands together. Together. Together.

'Check to see if any water comes out,' he shouts at Jess. He keeps pummelling. He shouts at the inert form. 'Come on, Kevin, you fucker. Breathe. Breathe. I got you out of that river, that fucking river, so I can beat you in a race, so I can race you up the mountain, so I can beat you. I am going to fucking beat you this time. Oh yes. Come on, you BREATHE. Please…breathe.'

With each shout, he pushes again and again.

'I see it. I see it. Water. From his mouth,' screams Jess.

The inert form of her brother coughs and water pours from

his mouth. He takes a huge gasping breath, and coughs again. Jess screams with delight, and as her brother and father appear, the fell-runner passes out with pain and exhaustion.

30: Winter storms

Wednesday 1st December

The late autumn storm clouds are racing in from the south-west. They come in bursts. The Lakeland Valleys beneath them are not sheltered from these storms. They soak all in their path. They spare no one. Not the walkers without their waterproofs or the stoic ewes wet and running with the rams, not the drivers on the A66 turning on their windscreen wipers, not the pupils down at the school moving between lessons. But, after the storms of the week before, they seem mild, almost benign.

Up on top of Latrigg, up with the buzzard, these storms clouds roll past, with showers, followed by sun, then showers again: the shafts of rain-soaked sunlight pierce the gaps. From across the world, people come to these mountains. They come to see the views that the weather and the people have created.

The storms come up from the south-west over the prison in Lorton Vale. As they hit the edge of the escarpment, they rise, and the rain starts. Here, the prisoner is in the kitchen, almost oblivious to the rain followed by the sunshine. At the beginning of the year, he was just another prisoner with a dark history. Now he is in love and in torment. The closer freedom comes, the more anxious he becomes.

As the storm moves up, it passes over the high reaches of the Newlands Valley where Jess's father and brothers are in the kitchen, having coffee as they take a break from clearing up the mess. Kevin has his arm in a sling and his face is covered with cuts and bruises. With each deep breath he winces with pain from his four broken ribs.

The storm moves onto the shepherdess, out in her fields with her dogs at her heels. She is checking her sheep as the storm passes on down the valley. She is caught in the rain, but she is a hardy soul and just turns her collar up. She has yet to tell all of her story, but she has seen her life change. She has danced closer to her two men, her prisoner, Steve, and her fell-runner, Ashley. Her hardened heart has opened up to them. She has shared music with Ashley, and she has taught him to dance.

As the storm passes down the Newlands Valley, it reaches Portinscale, on the outskirts of Keswick, where Hazel is in her car, about to show a client round a house. The man she loves is not married but a murderer. They have both finally unburdened their secrets. They both thought they would never find love again. But, now they have it, it has come with a bitter symphony of emotions.

Moving down the valley to the school Jess and the fell-runner are in their geography lesson. Jess steals secret glances at him, the man who saved her brother. Their thoughts hold each other and tango together while their bodies stay in the lesson. They have run together. They have fought together. They have danced together. She looks at his leg in a cast up to the knee. He fractured his ankle vaulting the pen. The doctor has promised it will be good by Xmas. Above all, they are in love and, like puppies, they have tested each other to see what reaction they get. But they keep coming back for more.

Ashley's year began with violence but now is ending in

happiness as the jigsaw pieces of his life fit into place. He runs because it feels so natural. To begin with, running was just something he did because he loved it, and now he can see his father and his father's father stretching back generations. He now talks of trying to find his father in Kenya. Running is in his blood and he wants to see where that blood comes from.

The flood waters of loneliness which permeated through Joyce, Steve and Ashley's lives have receded to be replaced by a rising tide of friendship, perhaps even love. Not all that it has revealed is happiness, not all stories are told. The flock is not so lonely now as the secrets are told.

31: Two women talk

Wednesday 15th December

'Watch somebody's face.'

Hazel looks intently across the table and continues her monologue.

'Watch somebody as they shop in the supermarket, talk on the phone, or chat to a friend. Their face is like the sea, always moving, never still. The waves of emotion and sentiment, of thought and reaction produce a thousand tiny changes in expression. Their mouth tightens. Their eyebrows rise and fall. The hint of a smile. The flaring of nostrils. The furrowing of eyebrows. And we humans read those expressions, the ripples and currents on the sea of sentiment that lies beneath.

'So when somebody's face stops moving, stops reacting, stops its continuous motion and becomes impassive, we notice. When people lose their facial expression, it is as if they stop speaking a language. And the rest of the human race notices those changes. When my face stops smiling, stops reacting, stops talking, my colleagues think I have become indifferent, alienated, and distant. They say to me to "smile – it may never happen" and I want to scream. It is happening. Right now, inside me.'

Hazel takes a sip of her coffee.

'I want to tell them. I want to ask; do they know what it's like to look in the mirror and see a mask? I know what I am feeling. I don't want to have a poker face. It's just that my face, without the drugs, doesn't show those changes. I want to ask them if they realise that my arm can feel like a headless chicken, flapping out of control. I want to tell them that my fingers can develop a life of their own. This little finger here will twitch uncontrollably as though it is no longer part of me.

'But I scream none of those things. I look at them and do my best to smile. I do my best to reboot my face, so it reacts the way it should.'

Hazel holds her coffee with both hands as she talks and looks down at the table. She is visiting the only person she can talk to, the only person who knows her and the prisoner. She has come to see the shepherdess.

Since the day she and Steve didn't walk or have sex, but shared their secrets, her mind has gone over and over the last few months. But the more she thinks, the less is anything clear. She badly needs to talk to someone to unburden her feelings. She has turned to the only person she can, the only person who knows both their secrets.

She drove past the shepherdess's farm three times before she plucked up courage to go and see her. Should she ring first? What would she say? *'I need to come and talk about my secret and his secret.'*

Ridiculous. Impossible. But each time she passes the farm entrance and drives on as her courage fails her, the need to talk builds up. And then, when the December frost is thick on the ground, she passes the farm one last time and sees Joyce in the yard. So, heart in mouth, in a drugged-up sea of emotion, she drives into the farmyard.

When they sit down for coffee, Hazel begins to explain and realises with an inward smile that while she is grappling with Steve's crimes, the shepherdess has known about them since day one.

'I didn't know. I didn't know till two weeks ago that Steve was a prisoner. I didn't know until then that he is a murderer.'

'And what was your reaction?' Joyce asks.

'I didn't know...my world...' Hazel struggles for words, 'my world fell apart.'

'...because you didn't know?'

'Yes and no. I knew he had a secret. I knew there was something funny about him. I didn't believe all that business that he was your son. I assumed he had a wife, that I was a bit on the side when his wife sent him off to walk the dog. Then, before we had sex for the first time, he promised me he wasn't married. At first I was relieved, but then I realised that he still had a secret. I just couldn't work out what it was.

'What he didn't know was that I had a secret too. I had my own reason for not wanting to get too close. But the more we walked, the more I realised that we were stuck not going forward or backward.'

Joyce looked up at Hazel's mention of a secret, and, as blunt as ever, asked:

'What is your secret?'

'I have Parkinson's Disease. I have a disease from which I will only get worse, never better.'

Joyce stares at her for a moment and says, 'Parkinson's Disease...of course, of course. I should have noticed. The lop-sided smile...the use of your left hand...your slightly stiff movements...'

Hazel looks at her in amazement. 'How do you know?'

'My father had Parkinson's for twenty years before he died. I watched him go...'

Joyce stops mid-sentence, realising that telling Hazel about how her father suffered is not a good idea. She changes tack.

'So, Steve discovered that you have Parkinson's, and you discovered that he was a prisoner.'

'Did you ever feel you should have warned me?'

Joyce pauses a moment, as the question has caught her off guard.

'No, to begin with it never occurred to me. I didn't know you. Had the two of us ever exchanged more than a couple of sentences? In September, I realised that the two of you were becoming serious. I told him he had to tell you. Should I have told you something directly? Maybe I should have said something.'

Her tone changes and she tries to reassure.

'I can tell you I have never felt threatened by him. I know what he did. He told me after a couple months what happened, but he had done. That's part of the rules with the prison. But I have never felt in danger or threatened. Indeed, while I didn't know him beforehand, he has always been very gentle, very thoughtful during all the time he has spent with me. I feel prison has done for him what it is meant to do. It has made him atone for his crimes. But none of this helps you. Where is your heart now? Now that you know?'

'To start with I was repulsed. I had...'

She cannot finish the sentence.

'...had sex with him? I can see how that might make you feel different.'

'Now my emotions have gone in every direction that could be imagined. Is he still the man I loved, I wanted? What has changed? One terrible night which he has done time for, which he will always have to live with, which he regrets.'

Her voice trails off, and then, re-energised, the new voice comes back.

'But then I think; it could be me. He could lose it with me and I would be next. He is a murderer. A murderer!' She almost shouts the last words.

'Once a killer, always a killer. Heh? Do you dance?' The shepherdess asks from nowhere.

Hazel is dumbfounded by this question.

'Do I dance?' Hazel is finding it hard to keep up with the twists and turns of this conversation.

'My dad found that dancing was one of the few ways he could unfreeze, that he could hold back the symptoms of Parkinson's. He was ill before today's modern drugs, and so he suffered much worse. Dancing helped. He could talk when he danced so my mother and I had to dance with him every night. It was the way my mother and he talked. They used to dance together and chat. It was so romantic, so terrible. I used to dance with him as well, when he wanted to talk to me or when he was pent up with the emotion of a day frozen in his body. I have always told people that I learnt how to dance as a debutante. But I learnt way before that. So for me dancing and talking go hand in hand. I have taught the young lad from Keswick School, who helps with the sheep, to dance. He has taught his girlfriend. Now I want to teach you because you need to talk, and you need to dance.'

Hazel is amazed by these words. But any road from her quagmire will do. Hazel stretches out her hand across the table, her eyes alive, and whispers, 'Please…please teach me to dance.'

The two women stand in the middle of the kitchen. Joyce puts on the music in the living room. She doesn't want to dance there with Hazel. She somehow feels that that is a special place reserved for her and the fell-runner. Joyce stands face to face with Hazel. The grey-haired woman puts her arm round the waist of the tall slim woman she faces.

'Dancing is all about channelling your feelings, your real feelings, into motion. In the days when young couples couldn't be alone together, formal dances were the only place they could meet. Indeed, the whirl of the dance floor was one of the few places they could be alone. So you have to imagine that the tango, which I am about to show you, is the closest many couples got to intimacy…to touching.'

She says that last word with such feeling, with such emphasis, that Hazel can only smile. She came here to talk, and has ended up dancing.

'Now, as I move towards you, I want you to walk away, matching my footsteps. And then I am going to stop walking but you keep going and when you get to the end of my arm's length, I am going to pull you back into my arms. That's it. That's it. Now let's try that again.'

As they practise, Joyce goes to the eye of the emotional storm.

'Do you love him? That's it, that's it, but with more grace, if I may say. Make this dance about passion, Hazel.'

Watching her feet, Hazel eventually responds, 'What is love?'

'That's not an answer. Okay, let's not give names to emotions. How does he make you feel? Do you miss him?'

'Oh yes, I miss him. During the week, in the days between Saturdays, I miss him. I think about him. There was a golden period when I didn't know that there was something I didn't know, if you see what I mean, when it seemed perfect. Even now, my heart races when we meet. I certainly find him very attractive. I want the physical him. I guess it's the emotional him that makes me wary.'

'Did you love him before you knew he was a prisoner?'

'I was on that road, I suppose.'

'Let's try another move. I am going to pull you in close and then lean towards you, and I want you to lean backwards as if to get away from me. Let me ask you another question. What does he think about? If I were dancing with him, what would he be saying?'

'I don't know. I just don't...don't know how he could love somebody who has what I've got. How could he love somebody, I mean how could anybody love somebody, who will be old before their time? How could he find me attractive?'

'You are so young and beautiful, aren't you? That's not a compliment. When you are young, it's all about looks, but over time it can't be. We all get old...no, no you've got to lean back further while I hold you – and one leg goes up to balance yourself...where was I? Couples have children. They get jobs. They are tired. He has got to love you for who you are today. You have got to love him for who he is today. I was listening to the radio the other day. It was about people's sex drive. They said that if you put a pebble in a jar for every time people had sex in the first year of their relationship, and then took a pebble out for every time they had sex after that, the jar, for most couples, would never be empty.

'For you and him to work, you...you have to want to be with him even when everything is mundane.'

They stop dancing and stand in the kitchen, looking at each other. Joyce's voice rises now.

'If I asked him what he thought, I think he'd be saying much the same as you. "I don't know what she feels. I don't know what to think." That is what is so brilliant. As you said, you knew he had a secret, and you had a secret. You are equals. You are falling in love. You are both young. You are both beautiful, and I would guess you are both sitting there, second guessing each other. The boulders on your road to love are a bit bigger than some, but every couple has them. Yes, you both have things about the other to come to terms with. But so does every couple. It's usually that "this habit drives me nuts. I hate the way she or he does this or that", but relationships are about compromise. Pure and simple. Compromise. Not holding grudges. And talking. And you two need to talk. You need to talk …and to dance.'

Hazel stands, not knowing what to say. She wants to believe what the shepherdess is saying. Wants to believe what she is being told. Wants to be guided to calmer waters, wants to be in love.

'Thank you. Thank you. Thank you for that emotional slap.'

'No need to thank me. Just love him. Make it work. It is too late for me. My chance has gone. I'll never know when I made the wrong call. For you, it is all to dance for.'

32: Another first dance

Saturday 18th December

After eleven months with Saturdays on Joyce's farm, Steve is allowed to take his visits one step further. He can stay overnight. This is the next step in easing prisoners back into the real world. If they show they can handle day release, then in due course, they can have an overnight stay and then a weekend release. This is Steve's first night release. His first night outside of prison in all these years.

The first night of freedom arrives. Joyce has agreed to pick him up so he doesn't have to carry all his night things on the bike in the dark. Night release starts at 5 p.m. and ends the next day at noon when Joyce will return him to the prison. Steve has no family who want to have him for night release, so Joyce has become his family, and he is going to stay with her.

She has promised him a night of treats and surprises. He has told her the food he would like; roast beef and banoffee pie, and lots of roast potatoes. He has asked if he can watch a DVD with her. He chooses one which he could never watch in prison because war films are frowned on – *Saving Private Ryan*. She has bought him his favourite beer and a huge pack of crisps. The evening is prepared. It is to be as normal as possible. This is night release normality. He has also asked if he can have a bath, impossible when the prison only has showers.

Joyce parks the car and they walk to the house together. Steve notices that Joyce is not being her normal self. He is puzzled. He is just about to ask her if she is all right when they come through the farmhouse door and Rose and Kipper greet him. He does not understand. What is Rose doing there?

He looks up and there is Hazel. He stares at her. He thought we would never see her again. She is sitting in a kitchen chair, but she doesn't move. She doesn't speak. Her face is expressionless. She just looks at him. Rose returns to the Aga. He takes a step forward, as if walking into a trap. Why doesn't she speak? He looks at Joyce as if for guidance. She just watches the scene, waiting for the next move. Finally, Hazel moves to speak. Her words come out, painfully, slowly, one by one, each forced out with effort and pain.

'This is me, Steve. This is me with Parkinson's and no drugs. I have sat here all afternoon. I have been waiting for you. Letting my drugs wear off. Letting my muscles seize up. Letting my mind think of all the questions I want to ask you, questions that I need to hear you answer. You see this – my mind has divorced my body. Without drugs, I seize up. Since that day we told each other our secrets, I haven't known what to think or what to do. Could I love you with your past? Could you love me with my future? I want you to tell me exactly what you did and why.

'And I want you to see me at my worst. I need us to start again, with you knowing the worst that you can know. And I need to hear the worst that I can hear. I need you to see what you are letting yourself in for.'

She pauses and turns her head towards the Aga and in a high-pitched yelp shouts, 'Rose!'

The dog is instantly on its feet and trots over to her mistress. Hazel lowers her face to meet the dog and the dog on back paws puts her front legs on Hazel's knees and licks Hazel's face. Hazel closes her eyes as the dog works. After a minute, Hazel's expression begins to return and her head loosens. Hazel yelps again and Rose stops and stands with her head next to Hazel's outstretched hand. Hazel's fingers clasp the dog's collar. Another yelp with the tone of a sleigh driver, the dog and Hazel pull together as one, and Hazel is up out of her chair.

Steve and Joyce can only stare at this scene, this bond between woman and dog. Hazel is standing now. She starts to speak again.

'Parkinson's is incurable. I can only get worse. I can have good days and bad days, but I can't have perfect days. On good days, when I get the medicine right, you would hardly notice. I am good, so good at hiding things now.

'You know that day on Maiden Moor, when we agreed to meet. I said I had gone down the other side of the hill and heard you; I was lying. One of the symptoms of Parkinson's for me is narcolepsy, falling almost instantly asleep. I was having a sleep in the heather when you heard me, and Rose did what she just did now and got me up. A lick on the face, in the eyes and up the nose, is a great way to unfreeze me.

'You know that time I sat down on our walk from Grange and I asked you to pull me up. I wasn't flirting. I was about to freeze. Notice how I always hold my left hand in my pocket as if it's glued there or it holds the lead. It's my left side that is worse and immobile. I always make sure that my left hand is busy, whether it is holding my cup of tea with two hands like I am cold, or holding Rose's lead, because when it has no job to do it tremors. The fingers dance, endlessly twitching, waiting, waiting for a job.'

She looks at him and stares right at his eyes, and holds up her hand.

'This is me, Steve. This is me. Can you love this?'

She eyes him, not wanting an answer, as she staggers to the kitchen worktop.

'One last party trick, courtesy of Joyce. Music, please. Dancing unfreezes me without drugs.'

Joyce presses 'play' on her CD player and suddenly the music of Take That fills the room. Steve watches as Joyce moves towards Hazel. Joyce takes Hazel's hand and puts her hand behind her back. As she begins, Steve thinks Hazel will fall, but she doesn't, because her legs start to work. And round that room they dance. They dance the tango. Hazel is pulled back and forth by Joyce. Now she moves smoothly with Joyce. Hazel is pulled in close by Joyce's dance moves. Her usual grace and beauty returns. He watches as they dance round him. The dogs are excited by the movement as the women circle him. And, as Hazel whirls, she asks him, drunk with adrenaline and movement; she asks him, reckless in the movement; she asks him –

'Can you love me? Can you love me like this?'

She doesn't wait for an answer. She has another question. As the dancing slows, she turns to face him. The mood changes. She looks at him and asks, 'Can I trust you? If we are to love each other, I need to know if I can trust you. I need to know if at the heart of our relationship will be my fear. My fear is that your anger will leave me the next victim. Now, I will take my medicine and you can see the change.'

Hazel leans over the kitchen counter and swallows some pills from a small container. She sits down and looks at him.

Steve is just about to speak when Joyce gets there first.

'When I met my husband, we never talked. We just loved, or

so we thought. But each time we had a bad feeling, each time we were cross or unhappy, we never spoke. We put our feelings in an anger sack. They never disappeared. They were just buried. When things went wrong, all those feelings and all that anger came spewing out. We used it to torment each other. Soon, the scale of those feelings, all that anger and hurt, each small in its own right, was too big, too, too, too catastrophic when we finally talked about them. This is how the little things became big things and the big things become lethal weapons in our relationship.'

Joyce is speaking now, not for either of them but for her. An old lady reprising the lessons of her life's regrets.

'You two are both young. You both have so much for each other. I want you to stay here until you have both got out every feeling. Already, since the day you talked for the first time, too much has built up. You must talk. Better still, you must dance and, while you dance, I want you to hold each other and talk.

'Here, Steve. This is how you hold her. Arm behind her back. Stand upright. Now you move back together. Follow my move. And stop. Now move back in the opposite direction.'

Hazel interrupts Joyce. 'Tell me, tell me what you did, Steve.'

Round the kitchen they move. The dance continues as they expunge their fears.

'Tell me what you did...I have to know.'

'I was nineteen. I had wanted to go to uni, but my parents wouldn't let me.'

He struggles to get the words out.

'I was training to be an accountant and this girl worked in the sandwich shop where we got lunch. She was younger than me, but much more experienced. I had never had a girlfriend. She started to flirt with me and I was flattered.'

He pauses for breath 'So this girl, Kylie, we had a date, and a kiss, and one thing led to another.

'In the midst of all that lust, she got pregnant. It wasn't what either of us wanted. But she wouldn't have an abortion. Her mother would go ape, she said. Besides, she said, it was the drudge of the sandwich shop or the baby. I was too young, too stupid, too weak, to stop her getting pregnant in the first place, and too weak to make her see how young we were.'

He glances up at Hazel, to try to gauge her reaction, but her eyes are fixed firmly on the floor. Her hands clasped to his elbows to hold her steady.

'So we had a baby, Zoe. And once the baby was born, two things began to happen, one wonderful and one terrible. The wonderful thing was the delight of falling in love with a baby. The joy, the wonder of bringing a small being into the world and bit by bit, piece by piece, smile by smile discovering what love is like.'

'And the terrible thing?' Hazel asks, her first words since he started speaking.

'The terrible thing was Kylie began to change. She loved Zoe but it didn't transform her. It didn't change the way she saw the world in the way it did for me. For her Zoe was as much jailer as liberator. She was too young. We were both too young. Kylie began to resent what the baby had done to her freedom. But she didn't take it out on Zoe, but on me.

'She teased me about all my failings. That she was looking for a bit on the side, a man who was big enough to satisfy her. She kept me as far from my baby as she could. She stopped me helping. She told me how useless I was at changing nappies, at feeding her with a bottle, at everything. She took all her anger out on me. For the most part I just took her blows of anger like a punch bag.'

'What did happen?'

'My anger, unlike hers, just built up. Anger at the situation. Anger that I was in this stupid flat with a nagging unhappy wife not at uni. My accountancy work mates just made it worse with their teasing. My mother was always round. She loved being a grandmother, but I was like a ghost to her.

'I came back one night and Zoe and I started to fight. Zoe started crying because of all the shouting. We both tried to get to Zoe first, and I pushed Kylie back, so I held Zoe, and she stopped crying. Kylie was livid. She shouted and tried to grab her back and we tussled. Kylie pulled Zoe again. She thought I wasn't going to let Zoe go, but I did. I let Zoe go. I let her go. But Kylie didn't have her. As she fell, Zoe hit her head on the corner of a table, and then there was silence.

'We both stared. Kylie screamed at me. Then I start hitting Kylie – again and again and again. At first she resisted then she stopped. I didn't stop punching her until she fell, hitting her head on the floor.

'I had killed them both. I killed them both. I killed them both…'

He takes a deep breath.

'I admitted everything. I didn't want leniency.

'I loved Zoe from the moment she was born. I loved holding her in my arms. I loved her smile when she saw me. I loved her gurgle and her chuckle when I bounced her up and down. And I had killed her, so I had to be punished.

'I was convicted of manslaughter for Zoe, and the murder of Kylie. I wanted to be punished.

'There will *never* be another night like that, I promise you. I have had twelve years to mourn, to grieve, to wonder – what if…? How could…? – again and again. Prison is not my punishment.

It's my place. My punishment is knowing that I killed them. I killed my daughter. I loved her, and I killed her. And at night they come back to haunt me. I see her in my dreams. Growing up. Going to school. Birthday parties. Hugs with her dad. She would be thirteen, fourteen now. What things most parents celebrate, they are my wounds, and, just as I think they have healed, I have another dream and the emotional wounds burst open again. There is no peace.'

Tears are trickling down his face. He is talking to the room. To the world. Gradually, as he talks, as she hears his pain, his remorse, her face turns to his, and the stiff dance of strangers, melts. Their bodies move closer. He is silent as they dance for a minute or two. Then eventually he says,

'Can I love you the way you are? The way you will be? I can love you forever. I love you for the person you are. Not...not the body you inhabit. I have learnt to treasure what I have now. After twelve years of solitude, I know so much more about what is important. I can love you. I do love you. But I don't know how I can convince you. But you are the only person I think about when I imagine my life outside.

'And for the first time, *something, somebody* has replaced my daughter in my dreams. When I wake at night, *you* are there in my dreams. You are the woman I dream of. When I wake at night and I can't get back to sleep, I imagine the two of us, old and grey, walking the easy paths of the fells, sitting by the fire.

'I can live with your disease, your illness, and your frailties. I know you aren't perfect, but God knows neither am I.'

This is what she needs to hear. And, as they dance, they slow down and their bodies move closer. The gulf has been bridged, the ice has been broken. They can try again. They can start again.

33: As a shepherdess watched

Thursday 24th December

It is Christmas Eve: silent night, holy night. But all is not still. Once again, in a farm high up in the Newlands Valley, a ewe is preparing to give birth. This story may be ending as it started. For this, too, is a cold night. This, too, is a night when no lamb should be born outdoors.

The ewe chunners. Birth is near. She twists her head skyward and chunners again. But back in the cold field, the views and the walkers and the narrow roads and the mountains are of no help to the chunnering ewe. She needs the shepherdess. She is a soft southern Suffolk; she needs a barn and some straw on a night like this. Just as before, help is at hand. The shepherdess is performing her evening round, part walking the dogs and part checking her flock. It is the dogs who discover her first.

Joyce leads the ewe into the barn and makes a pen for her. The dogs obediently follow. It is 9 p.m. and the end of a quiet Christmas Eve. No family is visiting. The shepherdess goes back inside and gears herself up for a long night of childbirth. Inside, her heart is sinking. She is too old, her hands too gnarled, her body too tired, her fingers too weak. Perhaps she is too old to be a shepherdess. And in the way people do when they are exhausted, she has imagined all the terrible ways in which this night could end before it has even begun. The lambs will be dead. Her hands will ache for days. The ewe will die. She sits, cradling her lukewarm cup of tea, staring into the middle distance of her kitchen. She remembers how this year began, and now she fears she knows how it will end.

She returns to the sheep shed. Nothing has happened. There are no lambs. There is no sign of a head and two soft feet poking out. She ties the head of the ewe tightly to the bars of the pen and with her knee she pushes the ewe into the corner with just enough room for her to feel with her fingers inside the uterus. She can feel the nose just inside the mouth of the swollen lips but she can't feel any feet. She moves the ewe forward and pushes her hand further inside – still no feet. She lets the ewe go and leaves the pen. The dogs who have been watching her sense her desperation and move to appease her by licking her hand.

She sits on a hay bale and stares at the ewe. She wishes on nights like this that she was still married, that she had a man who she could share her tough times with, who she could turn to when her energy and her age catch up with her.

Suddenly she realises – she can call Ashley.

Ashley can help. The end of the year is not the same as the beginning.

She goes back inside and searches for his number on her scraps of paper. It is 10 p.m. Most people might hesitate to ring somebody on Christmas Eve. They would worry that they might be settling down for bed, or out with friends, or doing a host of things that it would be rude to interrupt. But now the idea is in her head, she doesn't pause to worry about whether it is right or wrong to call him or what he might think. Ten years of living alone and a lifetime of always and only seeing the world from her perspective leaves little space for doubt. Because tonight, here, and now, what she needs is help.

She finds his number on a scrap of paper on her clipboard. She dials slowly, concentrating on each digit. It rings and she listens.

'Joyce?' he answers. 'What's wrong?'

His greeting throws her.

'How did you know it was me?'

'Your number comes up on my screen. What's the matter?'

'I have got a ewe about to give birth and nothing is happening and…and…' and her voice cracks. There is a pause and then in a high-pitched voice taut with emotion, 'and I can't do this anymore.' And then she stops again.

He has never heard her like this. She has always been so strong, so stoic, so tough, but now she is close to tears. In that moment, he realises how hard this must be and how much their relationship means to them both.

'I'll be right there. I'll be as quick as I can.'

He hangs up before his voice cracks too.

It is a cold Christmas Eve. He puts on all the layers he can find to prepare for the birth in that cold shed. He doesn't know what he can do. He has helped with the lambs, but never helped with lambing. He goes downstairs where his mum and sister are watching telly.

'I am just going out,' he broadcasts into the room.

'Where?' his mum protests. 'At this hour? With your leg?'

He contemplates lying. To see his mates? To see Jess? To go to midnight communion? He tells the truth.

'The shepherdess needs help with an early lambing. I don't know when I'll be back, and the doctor said the leg is fine now.'

Outside the house, he texts Jess, *Going to jc. Early lambing. Can u help xoxox.*

As he cycles his leg shoots with pain from his barely healed leg, she responds, *At midnight church. Will come soon as finished, xoxo J ps will bring her prezzie ok?*

He goes straight to the sheep shed, and Joyce is there sitting on a hay bale watching the ewe with a vacant look. He has never seen her look so tired and so dishevelled. Her face is hanging.

'Hi,' he calls, so she knows he is there.

With no small talk, no greetings, she speaks firmly, launches off with where her thoughts are.

'You'll have to do it. I don't have the strength. I don't have the strength in my fingers. I don't have the mental strength either. I can't do this anymore.'

He interrupts her. 'I can't do it. I have never done a lambing before.'

His uncertainty brings her up short and brings out her inner bossy old woman. 'Yes, you can. I know you can. You are young with strength in your fingers. I will talk you through everything.'

It is 11.15 p.m.

'You'll need to scrub up your hands and arms using the gel, and then we will pen her against the side rails. I have had a feel and I think it's only one leg that is back, so it's not that difficult.'

'I can't do this. I have never done this before.'

But protest is futile.

Ten minutes later, he is scrubbed up clean and she has lent him an old anorak to protect him from the worst of the mess of birth. He realises with a wince that it isn't her size and probably belonged to her ex-husband or her son. The ewe is tied by the head and the shepherdess is holding her with her knee against the bars so she can't move.

He approaches the pen. He tries to joke with her, but inside he is terrified. At heart, he is still just a city boy. Maybe, he thinks in desperation, his father was also a sheep herder as well as a runner. He kneels down. The fact that this is Christmas Eve and they are in a stable and she is a shepherd with a ewe about to give birth is lost on them both, but somewhere high, high up above, perhaps there is a God, and perhaps he is smiling at the way he has thrown these lost souls together.

'Now move your right hand to her vulva and gently part the lips.'

Inside his head he squirms. 'Push your hand inside till you can feel first the nose, and then run your fingers down the neck to find the shoulders and each of the two front legs. What can you feel?'

'I've got the nose. That was easy. It's almost popping out. The left front leg is there too next to the nose.'

A pause while his lips are taut, tongue between them, his total concentration goes to find the right leg.

'I have found the right leg but…it's pushed back.'

She nods sympathetically. 'That's what I thought; its leg is back. So, you need to pull its right leg forward so both legs are next to the nose. Can you do that?'

He cannot speak. His voice would come out broken with fear. But for her, for the lamb and the ewe, he knows he must overcome his fears. He nods.

'Right, you need to push the lamb back, and then when you have done that, you need to flip that right leg forward before her contractions push the lamb back to the vagina entrance. So, start by pushing the chest of the lamb back. You need to time it between the contractions. I will tell you when to go…okay, she's relaxed – push the lamb now. Now. Go. Push, push, push, gently but firmly.'

His arm goes in deeper and his elbow disappears into the ewe and his chin rests on her back. His face winces as the next contraction tightens around his upper arm.

'Now wait, wait, wait and keeping the lamb where it is, find the right leg and gently pull it forward. Have you got it?'

He nods and says very quietly, 'I think so.'

'Now, take both the front hooves and cup them against the nose. Now let the contractions do the work. You can pull gently if you like it. But if the nose and the leg are together the lamb should pop out like an enormous turd.'

He smiles at the use of that word by her, a woman who is normally so proper.

She sees him smiling and realises why.

'Well, I have to talk your language as you are so young,' she teases. He is relieved that she is relaxing.

As she says this, the nose emerges from the ewe, followed by the head and the front legs. The ewe is now doing the work and the lamb is being born. Seconds later the lamb falls out of the ewe and onto the straw. They both look with pleasure and relief.

'Unto us a lamb is born. Happy Christmas.' The voice comes from behind them, at the entrance to the sheep shed.

They both turn around, startled. Ashley speaks first.

'Jess! I had completely forgotten. How long have you been there?'

She is smiling broadly. There is love in her eyes. She reaches the pen and leans over.

'Enough time to see that my man is going to be a shepherd. Hello Joyce, I'm Jess. I don't know why we haven't met before. Happy Christmas, Joyce. Happy Christmas, Ashley.' Beaming broadly, she kisses them both in greeting. Her attention turns to the ewe, because, as a farmer's daughter, she too has been here before.

'Is it breathing? Are there twins? It looks quite small...'

'Happy Christmas, Jess. It's lovely to meet you, even at this late hour. Yes, she's breathing. Ashley, rub the lamb with some straw and then let the ewe do some work. Oh, Jess, could you pass us the iodine spray from the shelf?'

She pauses, as if not wanting to say the words that follow.

'Yes, I think there is probably a twin. I don't know if we should wait or not. What time is it? 12.30? Shall we sing a carol?'

'Would you like me to have a feel?' asks Jess.

They both look at her in amazement.

'I am a farmer's daughter,' she protests, 'not just a pretty face. I have been lambing since I was at primary school.'

Ashley looks at her with delight. He has been saved from doing the lambing by himself.

'That would be fantastic,' Joyce murmurs. She has a feeling that Ashley is indebted to her, no matter how unjustified, but Jess owes her nothing. However, she is grateful for her help, as she is fit and strong, and her hands will be able to do things that Joyce's old ones can never do.

Jess puts on another old anorak that Joyce has brought out from the house. She kneels on the straw next to Ashley.

The face of this girl, with whom he is falling in love and who is falling in love with him, is inches from his. Jess is concentrating and he is watching. He looks up at Joyce. He can see the tiredness. He can see the concentration on what Jess is doing. He can see the relief in her eyes.

'The lamb is breached,' Jess announces. Joyce groans.

'Right, I've got the head now and I am pulling it round. I have got one leg. I can't find the other. I need to push my arm further in.'

There is silence as Jess works. It lasts for minutes, maybe ten.

'Ash, could you scratch my nose. My free hand is filthy.'

'It's Ashley!' His fingers hover near her nose. 'Right?'

'Yes, Ashley.'

Ashley obliges, and then kisses her cheek.

'Did I ask for a kiss?' she pretends to complain.

'You two, get on with the job in hand, please,' Joyce butts in, and neither of the lovers are sure if she is joking or serious.

'Right, I've turned the lamb over, now I just need to move it the right way up.'

They wait in silence again. Neither dare say anything as Jess works. Neither can think of anything to say. Eventually, she announces, 'I think we are there. I am just going to try and pull the lamb out. It has struggled enough.'

They watch as her arm is slowly, gradually withdrawn from the ewe. As her hand is finally freed, they can both see the nose and the front legs of the lamb that she pulled out with her arm. Seconds later, the lamb is lying in the straw.

Joyce instructs Ashley to remove the mucus from its mouth and face. As they watch the lamb coughs and gasps its first breath, Joyce let the ewe's head go so she can start to lick her lambs and bond with them. The ewe is chunnering as she licks and nudges both lambs. Joyce squeezes the ewe's teats to make sure there is some precious colostrum, that first protective milk. Jess holds the lambs up to teat.

'Jess, I can never thank you enough,' Joyce says as they watch the lambs start to search for the milk from their mother. Her voice trails off and then returns choked with emotion, 'If you two hadn't been here, I don't know what I would have done.'

'It's been amazing,' Jess says, beaming at her. 'To be here on Christmas Day, helping both of you help a ewe give birth, is just amazing. Amazing.' Her voice trails off as well.

'Shall we go inside?' Joyce suggests.

They leave the lambs and the ewe in their pen. The ewe is

still chunnering, still nudging and licking, still mothering and protecting.

'Actually, I'm sorry, you two, but I am all gone. I am knackered and I need to go to bed. I can't offer you a bed because they aren't made up, but the sofa and the TV are all yours. Thank you again. Happy Christmas and good night.'

'We have a present for you,' says Ashley.

'Can it wait till the morning?'

'No, not really. I should say, she can't. Jess, bring her over.'

Jess goes over a cardboard box by the kitchen door and pulls from the box a collie sheepdog puppy, and passes it to Ashley.

'Here she is,' he says, and cuddles the sleepy puppy up to his chest.

'Joyce, after the floods, Jess's family said they wanted to give me a puppy as a way of saying thank you. I said I can't do anything with a puppy – much as I'd love to. Then I thought that with Queenie having died, and remembered that I did know somebody who might be able to use a sheep dog. So, I want to give her to you.'

Joyce stares at them. For a moment, they don't know whether she is happy or sad.

'Thank you both. I am too tired to say more. Come here, all of you.' At this point she chokes, and motions them over and in the middle of the kitchen, the three of them embrace. They all are silent. No words will do. The puppy snuggled in the middle, licks Joyce on the face, just at the moment that a tear would have trickle down her face. She can say no more. She kisses them both on the forehead and goes upstairs.

They look at each other and grin like children, allowed to stay up late on Christmas Eve – which, in many ways, is just what they are.

'Come on, let's watch TV and snuggle on the sofa. I don't care what's on. I have never cuddled on a sofa and watched TV with you before – not properly, at least.'

He is sure they have, but doesn't disagree.

'Oh, wait. I think somebody would like to join us.'

The puppy snuggles in the space between them, and again licks Ashley's chin. He smiles. Kipper, alone in his basket now, watches them as he has watched the whole evening's proceedings. The pair of them lie together. For a few minutes they talk. They kiss. Soon, the tiredness and the TV absorb their energy. Jess is the first to succumb to sleep. She has been talking, but stops mid-sentence.

For a few moments, the fell-runner sees everything. Sees the wonder of where he is and how his life has changed. He smiles as he realises he has wanted to sleep with Jess since the moment he first saw her. And now he is, but he never imagined it would be like this. He sees Jess next to him and the puppy on his chest. In his mind's eye, he sees the shepherdess asleep on her bed upstairs, fully clothed but boots at least still in the kitchen. He sees his mother and his sister, safely at home asleep in their beds. He sees the ewe settling down next to her lambs in the sheep shed. And, as they curl next to her protected from the wind and the cold, the ewe licks and nuzzles her twins.

The ewe chunners. Birth has come.